Quest
Copyright ©

Note from the authors and dedications

From Joanne

This book has been written with my great-niece during her summer visits. We first started it five years ago when she was nine. Although I had an idea for the overall book, that first summer we had the most fabulous time brain storming ideas for the adventures the characters would go on!

Following that, I turned those ideas into a story. Charlotte wrote a few sections which I incorporated into the fuller story and she also helped me with the editing as well as drew pictures of the characters – of course, now, five years on she is a teenager and she thinks those pictures are very child-like, but I love them! I hope to show you the pictures on social media but, I am sure, Charlotte will want to update them!

Charlotte, my darling, I love you and adore to the ends of the universe. Thank you so much for working with me on this story. You are so talented and creative.

I dedicate this story to Andrea, who would have been exceptionally proud that her granddaughter had inherited her artistic ability.

Also to Celeste, who has been on her own 'journey' the past few years, and I am grateful thanks for all the proof reading she did.

And to Kryssie, for her advice on doing the book cover.

* * *

Dedication from Charlotte

To Casey, follow your dream.

Acknowledgements

Many thanks to Portmeirion in Wales. This amazing resort provided the inspiration for the story. If it wasn't for Portmeirion there would be no book. Those that know this place will recognise where the inspirations have come from.

It should be pointed out, though, that the story is not directly set at Portmeirion, eg, it is an island in the book whilst Portmeirion is a peninsula, and many other details have been changed slightly, for instance, the island of Giftan is now Grifftan, but much of it remains the same— there is still a bell tower, still a dome, still a stone ship, although you can't turn the plaque on the lion statue and find a secret hiding place nor will the third stone corbel at the Colonnade move, so PLEASE don't try!

PART ONE:

Quest for the

Lost Crown

CHAPTER ONE

The Wishing Tree

"I'll show them! I'll show them all that I *can* be the Lyon-Lady one day."

Caron strode angrily down the steps from the Inn, her tawny mane flying back from her face as she sped away. She ignored her mother, Tegwen, calling after her.

Her family had been at a formal luncheon with council members at the Inn in Trinity Row. Although they'd been talking about adult stuff—which was sometimes quite boring—whenever Caron tried to say something, her father had ignored her. This happened so often, and not just today, that she'd finally had enough.

Caron was the daughter of Leolin, the Lord of Lyon Isle. They were members of the Lyon-people who shared the Isle with the Fairies, known as the Fae, and the Mermaids—the Merfolk. There were, of course, other creatures on the Isle, but they were the only species who could speak.

As she ran, Caron heard voices behind her, and worrying that someone was coming after her, the Lyon-girl quickly made the decision to take what she called the secret tunnel from the Inn into the woods. In reality, it was just a side exit which led to a bridge into the woods.

It was very brave of her to venture that way as it could be dangerous—she was allowed to go to most places on the Isle by herself, but not deep into the woods. There were lots of stories about a part of the forest called the *Wild Woods*.

But that was the crux of the problem—no-one, particularly her father, thought she was courageous enough. Every time she tried to show anyone, her half-brother, Graham, butted in and pretended it was his idea. Her father listened to Graham and took him to meetings, leaving Caron behind. She thought today was the day Leolin would finally listen to her—but instead her father had told her to run off and play.

She growled to herself, clenching her paws in frustration. "But Graham can't be the Lyon-Lord one day. That's my job."

Although Graham was older than Caron, he was the son of her mother, not her father. Graham's father had been Human so that meant her father, Leolin, was his stepfather. Even if she hadn't known this, Graham's dark hair gave him away. True Lyons were shades of gold, tan and orange, but Graham had dark brown hair like the Humans, who were their mortal enemy.

Hearing someone running after her, Caron flattened herself behind a large tree.

"Blast the child. Where did she go?"

Peering around the side of the tree, the Lyon-girl watched as her mother scurried down the road toward the port calling for her. Caron chewed a claw as she watched Tegwen stride through the village of Trinity Row. She knew it was wrong to run off like that, although they didn't usually mind her going to most places around the island— it wasn't like going to the mainland, where danger lurked— where Humans lived!

She loved her parents dearly but wished they would stop treating her like a baby. After all, she was a direct descendant of the heroic Lyon-man, Peryn, who had led the Lyon-men—as well as the Fae and the Merfolk— from the mainland, bringing them to the island they had named Lyon Isle. These ancestors had escaped from the Humans who had hunted them, caged them, and sold them as slaves.

It had been many centuries since they all landed on the Isle and had co-existed peacefully ever after, although none of the three species spoke much to one another—they all lived their own lives. While the Lyon-men lived in villages across the Isle, the Fae resided in the woods, and the Merfolk dwelt in the caves around the coast.

With her mother out of sight, Caron continued on her path, stopping when she reached the bridge. She took a deep breath. There were stories about crossing this structure—that horrible things would occur when someone stepped on it.

Caron jumped and cried out loud at a noise, then laughed at herself. "Stop it, silly. It's only a bird." She was very proud of her ancestor, Peryn, and hoped to be as brave as he'd been.

"Here goes." The Lyon-girl took a step onto the wooden structure spanning the hill from the village to the woods, and then another, trying to step quietly. Nothing happened. Feeling confident she walked all the way over the bridge until she was on the other side—in the woods!

What was that silly story about? she wondered. As Caron glanced back over her shoulder she gasped. The bridge had turned golden! But moments later it changed into a very normal wooden bridge. She blinked and shook her head, thinking she must have imagined it.

"Well, I'm in the woods now. I've done something brave already and crossed the bridge." As she walked up the path she began to feel proud of herself. "Wouldn't it be good if I could do something to help my people like Peryn did?" She bit her lip and considered this. The question was, what could she do?

As she daydreamed about great daring deeds—fighting off dragons—rescuing maidens from sea monsters—and other such creatures which only existed in stories, she didn't notice that her walk had taken her further and further into the woods, up the slope of a hill.

Suddenly the Lyon-girl stopped short as she saw something that looked like the elusive white Unicorn. It suddenly crossed her path before disappearing into the woods.

"Was that what I thought it was?" she said to herself, trembling at the near contact. It was so rare to come across one of these creatures that no-one was sure they actually existed. Those that did mention seeing it were often drunk and so their tale was discounted.

The Lyon-girl looked around her, suddenly being aware she had come quite far. "Where am I?"

Caron turned swiftly and squinted back at the way she had come. There was a clear path leading back down to the bridge and the village. Happy she could find her way home again, the Lyon-girl sat on a large fallen tree in a clearing. Spring bulbs were growing quickly. The ground was awash with purple, yellow, and white flowers.

It was very peaceful. There were no sounds of Lyon-men moving about doing their work, no one calling for her or shushing her when she wanted to talk. Just an occasional song-bird, some rustling of wind through the trees, and the scampering of rabbits in the undergrowth. She sighed deeply, but her thoughts went back to her troubles.

Frustrated, she slammed a paw on the tree. "I wish my father would listen to me, instead of dismissing me because he thinks I am too young."

Just as Caron said this, a rumble came from beneath her.

"Whatever is that?" Placing her paws on the tree trunk, Caron could feel a vibration getting stronger and stronger.

As the tree shook, the noise got extremely loud causing the Lyon-girl to clap her paws over her ears.

Suddenly, with a loud roar, the tree ripped apart and broke into two halves. Caron yelped as she fell to the ground, and swiftly glanced around her in fear as she wondered what was going to happen next.

Jumping to her feet anxiously, she scurried backward a few paces for safety. Caron was fascinated and alarmed at the same time.

Her heart was pounding painfully in her chest as the noise began to stop. Leaves fluttered to the ground and the Lyon-girl brushed some stray petals from her orange tunic. "Gentle Goddess Friga!"

She finally felt safe enough to step forward. Despite what her father thought, Caron *was* a brave child—and a curious one, too—and she really wanted to look at the tree.

"Well, that's strange," she said out loud, for there were lots of symbols written on the tree, where it had fallen into two halves.

She peered closer but frowned when she realised she couldn't read it. It appeared to be various pictures. Caron could make out a butterfly, followed by a leaf. *I think that's a star*, she thought. Then, *A flower, for sure*. Next symbol was a feather. And, *was that a waterfall?* Caron gave up trying to decipher the rest and shook her head.

"Whatever does it mean?"

CHAPTER TWO

The Prophecy of the Lost Crown

"It's fairy language."

As the Lyon-girl swiftly turned around to face her, Nia hid behind the tree again, trembling in fear. She had been picking berries when the other girl had arrived and quickly hid out of sight of the scary Lyon.

Nia was a member of the fairy people—the Fae. They never talked to the Lyon-people or went anywhere near them. The Lyons were just too intimidating.

Why did I say anything? Nia looked about anxiously. Could she escape without being noticed?

"Please come out," pleaded the Lyon-girl who had caused the wishing tree to split.

Oh, fairydust! She heard me. Peering out timidly, Nia was so scared she was ready to wet herself, but the other girl didn't look as if she was about to pounce on her...yet!

"I won't hurt you, whoever you are. What's your name?"

Nia's legs were still shaking fiercely, but still the Lyon-girl sounded nice. Tilting her head to one side she noticed that the other creature was beckoning her. Staying where she was, the Fairy responded with a quiet stammer. "M—my name is N—Nia. I'm a Fairy."

The Lyon-girl landed on the ground with a thump. Nia wasn't sure if her stunned expression was from landing heavily or from meeting a Fairy. Not that she could understand why that would astonish a creature who was twice her size.

"Wow. I knew there were Fairies in the woods, but I've never met one. I'm Caron. I live in the Castell. My father is the Lyon-Lord. Where do you live? Don't you get cold in the woods?"

Smiling softly at all the questions from Caron, Nia finally felt brave enough to come out, although she didn't go too close. Caron might be just a Lyon-child, but even sitting down she was still bigger than Nia. "No, I don't get cold."

She studied Caron, thinking it a strange query since the Lyon-girl had thick fur and wore clothes—a sturdy tunic and leather boots.

Caron smiled back. Nia gasped and nearly fled since it looked like the Lyon-girl was baring her teeth. However, despite trembling fiercely, she resisted running away. There was something about the other girl that she liked. Besides it was very unusual for the Lyon-men to come into the woods.

"Look, can you tell me what this says?" The other girl indicated the writing on the tree.

Nia's trembles began to abate. "Oh, that's easy," she said in a soft voice. "There's a prophecy that tells of the lost crown of the Lyon-Lords and that the Humans will be defeated when the crown is found and worn by the rightful ruler of the Isle." She surprised herself saying so much. She was rather shy, even amongst her own people.

The Lyon-girl gasped and jumped to her feet to bend over the tree, looking at the words again. "Really? It says all that?"

Nia giggled. She was beginning to feel quite comfortable around the other girl. "No. We Fairies just know about the tale."

Caron glanced over her shoulder. "Oh, can you tell me about it?"

The Fairy shrugged. She thought a Lyon would know all about it. "So, did you know the Lyon-Lords had a crown?"

Shaking her head and frowning, Caron said, "No, but now you mention it I've seen pictures."

"Well, it was lost. No one knows why. But one day the Humans will find us here—you do know that they are bad, don't you?"

Caron grunted. "Yes. My half-brother, Graham, is part Human."

Nia didn't say she knew of him. Her Uncle Rees, the ruler of the Fae, occasionally spoke to the Lyons, but her people stayed well clear of Caron's brother as he had a reputation for nastiness. "It is said they will come looking for us one day and can only be defeated when the crown is found and is worn once more by the ruler of Lyon Isle—the Lyon-Lord, that is."

"Oh, he's my father!" exclaimed Caron, but then she frowned looking very fierce. "But he doesn't have a crown."

The Fairy was ready to run as the Lyon-girl was now looking rather scary, but bit her lip instead as she quietly said, "No, because it's lost."

Opening her eyes widely in amazement, the Lyon-girl asked, "So how do we find it?"

"Ah. It is said that the wishing tree would tell you where to look for the crown."

Caron gestured back to the split tree. "This is the wishing tree?"

"Hmm. Yes," said Nia. "I've never seen it break like that though!" She'd often wondered why it was called a wishing tree when no amount of wishing had made it do anything for her.

She stepped closer to look at the words, forgetting her fear of Caron who moved to kneel beside her, both of them studying the writing.

"Okay. So, what does *this* say?" The Lyon-girl gestured at the symbols that had appeared in the split in the tree.

The Fairy looked at the writing. "Go to the waterfall," declared Nia as she glanced up at Caron. Her eyes widened as the implications set in. "Do you think that's where the crown is? I mean, you did wish something about your father, and he is the Lyon-Lord."

Caron grabbed hold of Nia's arms and swung her around. "Yippee! We've found the crown!"

Nia was so excited she wasn't worried about the fact that she had just been embraced by a Lyon. "Well, we haven't found it yet. And anyway, we have to work out where the waterfall is. It could be anywhere. This is a big island."

Settling the Fairy back on her feet, Caron made a face. "You're right."

Thinking hard, Nia stated, "So there's a small one at the far end of Trinity Row, just inside the woods."

"Ooo. Let's go there now!"

Nia crossed her arms. Caron was clearly very impulsive in nature. "That waterfall dries up very quickly and I am sure there is nothing to see behind it."

Caron crouched down resting her elbows on her knees and cupping her chin in her paws as she thought. Her eyes suddenly lit up and Nia guessed the Lyon-girl had an answer. "I've thought of one. It's in Lady Square. Oh, but that's only a fountain. Not a waterfall. Don't suppose that counts."

The girls slumped back into thinking positions, Nia resting a hip against the split tree.

She nearly jumped out of her skin when Caron shouted "Portmer! There's a waterfall by the lake near the fisher-folk cottages."

"Yes. I know about it," cried Nia, equally excited, her bangles tinkling as she clapped her hands.

Caron grabbed Nia's arm. "Let's go there now!". She actually pulled Nia a little way before she abruptly halted, causing Nia to plough into the Lyon-girl's leg, her pale violet dress swirling about her. "Oh, sorry. I've just realised it's getting late and I'm already in trouble. If I go back to Portmer someone—my mother or somebody— may find me and tell me off. It's better for me if I go straight home."

Nia was disappointed but also intrigued about what Caron had done to get into trouble. But she didn't dare ask.

"Will you meet me there tomorrow?" asked Nia's new friend. The Fairy nodded eagerly, pushing a lock of light brown hair streaked with golden highlights back behind her ear. "When the clock strikes ten?" Although Fairies didn't use clocks, Nia knew what Caron was referring to. The sound of the clock chiming from Trinity Row could be heard at the edge of the woods.

"Until then. Bye."

As Nia watched the Lyon-girl walk down the hill and out of sight, she shook her head wondering if it had all been a dream. But when she looked again the wishing tree was still split in half.

"I did it! I spoke to a Lyon-girl and we are going on an adventure together!"

CHAPTER THREE
The Waterfall

It was early morning and Braith was quietly watching from the lake near some fisher-folk cottages. Being a Merboy—a member of the Mermaid people—he was naturally in the water but kept himself mostly hidden with the waterline just up to his eyes. His people could walk on the land, but he had never worked out how. It was something that happened when his people were around ten years old. However, most Merfolk didn't like walking up steps, so they rarely ventured further than the sands around the Isle, which was a shame as the Lyon villages were all brightly coloured and looked beautiful from a distance. He really wanted to explore them.

The Merboy was an excellent swimmer and often swam up streams going inland, using his powerful tail to leap over rocks where the water flowed, to emerge into ponds in the woods where the Fae lived or in places like the mill pond where the Lyon people dwelt so he could study all the other people with interest.

It was a Fairy and a Lyon-girl that he was watching now, and was very intrigued by them. He let himself sink down and quietly swam to the other side of the lake near the two strangers, so he could listen to them.

"Well, we are at the waterfall, so where do we look now, Nia?" said the Lyon-girl, who looked like many of the Lyon-people he had seen before—tawny-coloured fur, wearing a tunic and boots. She rested her paws on her hips—she had long claws he noticed.

"I have no idea, Caron. The writing just said, 'Go to the Waterfall,' replied Nia, the Fairy with a sigh. He studied the smaller of the two girls observing that the Fae always went barefooted and wore pastel-coloured clothing, unlike the more vibrant red, brown or orange hues of the Lyon-people. He smiled. His people wore no clothes, naturally, but the green and blue colours of their tails and hair were probably equally fascinating to the other folk.

"Hmmm. Do we have to get into the lake?"

Braith grinned at the Lyon-girl's words. He knew Lyons hated the water as they couldn't swim.

He ducked out of the way as the two girls moved closer to peer over the edge.

"I thought I saw something," Nia cried.

Braith sank further back into some reeds, trying to avoid swishing his tail and creating ripples, but it was hard as he was a little nervous, unsure if he should show himself.

The Lyon-girl used one paw to swish the lake as she scrutinised the water. "Where?"

"It's gone now." Nia slumped onto the bank.

Caron looked thoughtful. "It's a very large lake and we don't know how deep. I don't suppose you could fly over it to search for crowns or something glinting, as it will be made of jewels and gold, I imagine?"

Nia giggled. It was a light almost musical sound. "No. Fairies don't actually fly." She turned around. "Look, we don't have any wings."

Braith raised his eyes. That was news to him.

"But what about all the pictures of Fairies flying around?" queried Caron, who sounded as surprised as the Merboy.

Nia shrugged. "I guess it's because we are so small and light it can seem like we flit around."

"Well, it doesn't help us now. Neither of us can fly or swim."

For some reason Braith decided to speak up. "But I can—swim, that is."

The two girls jumped to their feet. The Fairy hid behind the Lyon-girl.

"Who's that?" cried the girl called Caron.

Braith swam forward. "Just me—Braith."

Caron gasped. "You're a Merboy. I've heard of you. Wow. In just two days I get to meet a Fairy *and* a member of the Merfolk."

He grinned. "I've never met a Lyon-person before, either. So, what are you two looking for?"

The Lyon-girl took charge, telling him about the prophecy of the lost crown while the Fairy nodded her head, still staying a distance away but no longer hiding behind the bigger girl.

"So, we came where the writing said to come," finished Caron. "This is great, having a Merboy on our Quest. You can look in the water where we can't go. Can you see any crowns?"

Braith was crestfallen. He was very familiar with the lake and knew there wasn't any crown hidden away. He told them this. "Are you sure it is *this* lake?"

"Yes," said Caron, crestfallen. "This is the only proper waterfall we know of."

Nia then spoke up, her quiet voice making it a little hard to hear her. "What about *behind* the waterfall?"

"I'll go," cried Braith, when he realised what the Fairy had said, and in a flash he swam through the waterfall, the water thundering in his ears. He stopped and shook his head. Looking around him, he could see there wasn't much, and he grimaced. He had been hoping there would be a crown lying around on the narrow ledge that ran from one side of the waterfall to the other, but no such luck.

He then glanced up and saw a rock shelf half way up the back wall over which the water fell. Determined to do this and take a crown back to the other two, he pulled himself on to the ledge. He was rather precariously perched, and it took a few moments before he felt brave enough to reach up, but the shelf was still too high up and he slithered back into the water with a splash.

"In all the seas!" he exclaimed in annoyance.

For once he wished he could get his legs. With a sigh he swam back through the waterfall and told the anxiously waiting girls, "There is a rock shelf behind the water. I couldn't reach it, but you might be able to if you could get past the waterfall. There's a narrow ledge running around the edge."

Nia stayed back, obviously frightened of being washed into the lake.

"That's okay. I'm strong," said Caron. Despite being clearly scared of the water, she bravely took a step into the waterfall, her back hugging the rockface.

"Keep going," yelled Braith as he swam through the pounding fall of water. He wasn't sure if she heard but a moment later, the Lyon-girl appeared.

Caron was very wet and fell to her knees coughing heavily.

"Careful. Don't fall in."

"I'm all right." The Lyon-girl sat back on her heels. "Where is this shelf?"

Braith gestured upward. "Over there."

He watched as Caron tentatively stood up and edged her way cautiously along the ledge. When she was underneath the shelf, Braith could see she was still too short.

"Can you reach up over your head and feel along the shelf?" he asked anxiously.

Caron did as he suggested while Braith held his breath. Then the Lyon-girl shouted with glee, "Found it!"

"Really? You found the crown?"

"No, but I've got something else. Let me get outside again."

Braith swam quickly back to Nia and they waited for Caron to reappear. The Lyon-girl flopped down to the ground and opened her paw.

She had a key!

"What's it for?" asked Nia after a moment's silence when they all looked at their find.

"I have no idea." Caron seemed to be as bewildered as all of them.

Suddenly, Braith had a brainwave. "I know of a hidden chest in a cave. The other Merkids have often wondered what was in it. I'm *certain* this key fits. The same symbol is on it as is on the chest—look at the starfish!"

The Lyon-girl jumped to her feet as she held out the key. "That's amazing. Where is this cave?"

Braith's excitement evaporated. "You guys can't get to it as it's around the other side of the Isle and you can only get to it by the sea."

Caron's expression fell.

Then Braith slapped himself on his chest and cried, "But I can go!"

The Lyon-girl glanced at Nia then back at Braith. She seemed rather reluctant to give up the precious key.

Biting her lip, she slowly unfurled her paw. "Well, if you think it is the right chest."

Braith grabbed the key. "It's guarded by an octopus. I'm sure I can get past him, though. I am the quickest swimmer of my people."

Before they could stop him, he dived down to the bottom of the lake to an underground stream that led back to the sea, his long turquoise green hair floating back and he swam swiftly. This was great. Despite having lots of Merchildren his age, he wasn't close friends with any. He wasn't sure if he was more excited by having two new friends or going on a Quest.

CHAPTER FOUR

The Cave of the Octopus

As Braith approached the cave of the octopus, all his courage left him. He'd felt quite confident when boasting to his new friends, Caron and Nia, that he knew where to find the chest the key fitted, but as he swam toward the entrance he warily looked about for signs of the octopus. His heart was thumping so hard he was sure the creature would be able to hear it.

Although other Merchildren dared each other to come to the home of the eight-tentacled sea creature, they all knew how dangerous it was, for an octopus could easily capture a Merchild. That's why it was such fun to taunt it and swim away, as Merfolk were exceptionally fast swimmers.

His grandmother warned him the creature would catch him one day and gobble him up. Braith didn't believe that would happen—at least, he thought it was just a tale!

But just in case, he entered stealthily, trying to swim with as little movement as possible to avoid any ripples in the water that would give him away to the octopus if it happened to be inside.

The cave was only accessible by swimming underwater and coming up into a pool in the middle. He swam slowly until just his eyes were above the water and looked around swiftly.

So far so good.

There was no sign of the creature and, despite being a cave, it was very bright. The Merboy grinned. The octopus was known for loving pretty things and the cave was full of bright metal objects lying around on the sand at the back of the cave as it sloped upwards.

Braith swam in that direction and pulled himself onto the higher ground with a heave, pushing aside some of the treasure so he wasn't sitting on it. As the octopus was nowhere in sight, he rummaged quickly through everything, hoping to find the crown before the creature came back. There were heaps of coins, a buckle, a spoon, a tankard, some necklaces, earrings, and bangles, a few swords and daggers. He picked one up and pretended to wield it with a chuckle.

"Hey, Mr Octopus, take that!"

Then he discarded it to look at the rest of the items. There were shoes, clothing, rope, a ship's compass and even a ship's wheel—all things obtained from shipwrecks or thrown away. He picked up a pretty pearl-decorated comb thinking it was a pity the girls were not with him as they would probably have liked that.

But there was no crown. He grunted in disappointment.

Then Braith remembered he was looking for something on which to use the key. "You fool. Okay, where was that chest?" He was sure he had seen a small, brightly-decorated container when he had been brave enough to venture into the cave one day.

Glancing around he noticed a passage leading to another cave. *Oh yes. It's back there.* Flipping over he jumped back into the water but in his eagerness, there came a loud splash.

Uh oh! He stayed still wondering if the ripple in the water would warn the octopus if it was nearby.

A few seconds went by, then some more. Braith's nerves calmed a little.

When all seemed quiet the Merboy slowly swam to the passage and poked his head through to the next cave.

There it is! The chest he recalled from a previous visit was on a low golden table at the far side where the water was shallow. Braith's grinned in excitement and without another thought he darted inside. But just as Braith reached out to touch the chest, he got squirted. The octopus had hidden out of sight protecting his loot from intruders.

"Ahh!" the Merboy cried. His ear had been filled with black ink that octopuses squirt. It was thick and thoroughly yucky.

Scurrying backward out of reach of the creature, Braith hit the far wall. He needed a plan—quickly! Raising his fists to somehow fight off the creature, he realised he still held the key in one hand, and the pearl comb in his other and an idea came to him.

"Yoo hoo!" he called, waving the comb in the air. That got the octopus's attention and before it came toward him, Braith quickly threw it in the other direction away.

His ploy worked, and the creature scuttled after the item, clearly not aware that it already belonged to him.

Braith didn't want to waste time opening the chest, so he swiftly snatched it and swam back into the first cave. As he started to dive down under the water to exit the cave he felt something grab his tailfin.

No!

Fighting spirit came over him and he wriggled fiercely, managing to free himself just as another tentacle snaked around his wrist—the one holding the precious key he needed to open his stolen goods! Holding the chest tightly against his body with his free hand, Braith gave an almighty slap with his tail, causing a big wave in the water which splashed over them both. Amazingly, it worked…and he was suddenly free! Diving down as fast as he could, he darted from side to side, narrowly keeping ahead of the chasing octopus whose tentacles reached out to seize him, only to find the Merboy had eluded him.

But Braith couldn't keep this up for long. His chest was heaving with exertion and just as he was wondering how he was going to escape the octopus, a school of fish came by catching Braith in their midst. Startled at first, then he couldn't believe his luck. As they swarmed away, taking the Merboy with them, Braith glanced over his shoulder and saw the octopus was blinded by the fish, striking out in frustration, trying to grab anything it could. He felt sorry for the fish caught in the creature's fury, but very glad he had got away.

After a short while, when he felt it safe, Braith swam away from the fish. Happily, the octopus was nowhere to be seen. Clutching the chest in delight, he twirled around. *I did it! I did it! I did it!*

The Merboy had to stop after a while as he began to feel sick—partly because his head was spinning from his movement, but also because he began to feel mean stealing something from the octopus. He vowed to find some flotsam washed up on the beach and leave it for the creature. But he'd do that another day. For now, he made his way to the shore, so he could open it, eager to return to the girls. He grinned at the idea of wearing the crown when he met them.

"That would be a laugh."

CHAPTER FIVE

The Crown

Nia couldn't contain her excitement and jumped around as Braith placed the chest before them. The girls had spent a long hour waiting for the Merboy to return, all the while keeping out of sight of the Lyon-people who lived in the fisher cottages nearby. They had discussed what the crown might look like, both deciding it would be covered in jewels but not agreeing whether it would be gold or silver. Well, it had mostly been Caron talking with Nia listening. She was still stunned by the fact that she was on an adventure with not only a Lyon-girl but a Merboy, too.

"Now, I have already opened it," Braith told them as he unlocked the chest, "and it's not what we thought was inside."

"What? Why not?" growled Caron causing Nia to jump at the sound. She was getting used to the Lyon-girl but occasionally Caron still startled her.

"You'll see," said Braith enigmatically.

The two girls bent over as the Merboy lifted the lid. The chest was smaller than Nia had been expecting. She had in mind a box that was as big as she was.

She peered inside and yipped as she saw something glittery like a crown. *What was Braith going on about?*

Then she looked again. "Oh no!" she cried as she looked in dismay at the other two. The chest contained a crown all right, but it was broken.

Caron reached in and picked it up, turning it about as the three examined their find. It was gold after all and glittered in the sunlight. There were all sorts of coloured jewels studding the metal, but it wasn't a whole crown.

"I thought we could find it and put it on." Nia could hear the disappointment in the Lyon-girl's voice.

As they all looked at what Caron held, Braith asked, "How would it go on your head?"

The Lyon-girl lifted it up over her head, and they could see it was a side part—or a front part. A section, whatever, and there seemed to be clips at the side but she wasn't sure what they would be for.

As the girls slumped to the ground beside the water, Braith put his forearms on the bank and rested his chin on them. "So that's that! End of our Quest. We can't exactly give this to Caron's father. He'd look stupid sticking it on his head. The Humans would just laugh at him. Hey, maybe that's how they will be overcome. They will giggle themselves to death." Braith then splashed about in the water pretending to die laughing.

Caron reached over and thumped the Merboy on his shoulder to get him to stop his jesting and Nia rolled her eyes.

"Are you sure there wasn't anything else in there? You might have missed it," asked Caron gruffly.

Braith was clearly annoyed. "No! That was all there was."

"Sorry. Didn't mean to growl at you. But the prophecy said we must have the crown to defeat the Humans. That's right. Isn't it, Nia?"

The Fairy nodded at Caron.

"So, is it worth going back to see if there was anything else in the octopus cave?"

Nia bit her lip at Caron's useful suggestion and they both looked at Braith who grimaced.

"Do you realise how dangerous that octopus was? I barely got away with my life."

The Fairy thought the Merboy was being somewhat dramatic but didn't like to say so.

"Anyhow, there *were* other things in the cave..."

Before he got a chance to finish, Caron jumped to her feet. "Maybe if I go, I can scare off the creature."

Braith snorted. "Don't be daft. Lyons can't swim, and you must dive under the water to get inside. However, I did look through all the other treasure in the cave. There were lots of necklaces and coins and stuff but no other crowns."

The threesome was stumped as to what to do next. Caron tried rubbing the piece they had in the hope it would magically make the rest appear. Nia meanwhile tried saying something in Fae. Braith just looked sadly at it.

Caron then jumped to her feet and paced up and down. "Okay. So, let's think logically. The tree split when I made a wish and the words said to come here to the waterfall. Yep?"

The other two nodded.

"And when we came here we found the key hidden behind the waterfall, so it makes sense that the key is linked to the prophecy. Do you agree?"

Nia and Braith both said, "Yes," at the same time and laughed.

The Lyon-girl stopped and turned to them. "So, if the key fitted into that chest," she said gesturing to the open casket lying abandoned on the ground, "and all we found in there was this bit of crown, it means this is the *right* crown so there must be *more* pieces."

There was silence as they all took that in. Then Braith whooped and jumped back in the water, causing a small wave to go over the bank. The girls screamed but Nia grabbed hold of the crown before it slid into the lake.

"Sorry." Braith was suitably ashamed.

They settled down again and Caron declared, "That all makes sense now. It can't be that easy or it wouldn't be a proper Quest."

Braith groaned. "Okay guys, so where are the other pieces?"

That brought them down to earth. They pondered what to do next. Braith took hold of the chest turning it over and poking to see if it had any loose parts that might be further clues. But no success. The Lyon-girl had already gone behind the waterfall whilst Braith had gone in case there were other keys, but the shelf was empty, and Caron just got wet again.

"Do you think it would help if you guys went back to the wishing tree again?" suggested the Merboy.

"That's an idea," pondered Caron. However, as she had to get home soon, or she'd miss her lessons, the Lyon-girl said she would go back to the wishing tree another day but for now the question was where should they keep this piece? She didn't dare take it home in case her half-brother Graham found it. Nia couldn't as she was sure her uncle, the Fairy-King, would sense it. Braith was similarly worried that one of the Merfolk would find it.

"I know!" Caron excitedly jumped up and down, startling the other two. "I know of a secret place to hide the crown!"

CHAPTER SIX

The Secret Hiding Place

Caron looked furtively around, listening hard for any Lyon-men who might be in the vicinity of her secret hiding place. Her hand trembled as she clutched the crown under her tunic and turned toward the meadows. Part of her wished Nia and Braith were with her, but that wasn't possible in the middle of the Lyon villages.

She had walked up the steep hill from Portmer. If she had gone straight ahead she would be in Trinity Row. *Where the Quest started,* she thought to herself, smiling as she recalled all that had happened since storming out of the Inn yesterday leaving her parents behind. She had sworn then she would do something to show them. The Lyon-girl giggled. "If only they knew."

Her voice sounded loud in the empty lane that led to a quiet area between the villages and she jumped before realising it was only herself. She was aware that she couldn't tell her parents what she had been doing. Not until she and her friends had got the crown back together.

Quickly scurrying on, Caron drew her tunic further over the piece of the crown they had found, and hugged it to her body, keeping it safe before venturing into the meadow. Her goal was the statue of a lion in the herb gardens. A year or two before, she had discovered there was a secret hollow place inside.

As she neared her destination, she swallowed a gasp as she heard footsteps. *Gentle Goddess Friga!*

Ducking behind the mill, Caron plastered her body in an alcove against the side of the building, hoping that Graham hadn't seen her.

Her brother and three of his friends came walking past and the Lyon-girl held her breath, still trying to blend into the shadows.

"So, Graham, how did you come to get the honour of leading the Spring Procession?"

What?! Caron was so stunned by what Graham's friend had said, she nearly spoke out loud. How on earth had her brother been given that task? It was usually done by a member of the Lyon-Lord's family—a full member! Then she felt guilty. Graham was her brother after all, even if he wasn't her father's son. She frowned at the people Graham was with. She couldn't really say they were his friends as he didn't have any. No, these were Lyon-boys who wanted to be *in* with the big kids.

From where she was hidden, she heard Graham chuckle. "Mother had an argument with my stepfather. He wanted her to lead the parade, but she said it should go to Caron this year. However, Leolin said my sister was too young. At which point he turned to me and said I should do it."

Thankfully her brother and his friends had moved on because Caron sank to the ground crying at those words. She was pleased her mother had stood up for her but was upset at her father.

Then she pounded a paw against the ground. "Why won't he see that I *am* old enough?"

Her anger burned off her tears and she jumped to her feet.

"I'll show him. I really will."

Running to the statue, she wiped her wet face with the back of a paw and then tried to calm herself and think clearly. It had been a while since she had been there, and she had to remember how to open the hidey-hole. Reaching out with both paws, she took hold of the circular plaque which was on the base.

The statue had actually been created to honour the very first Lyon-Lord, Peryn, and there were words inscribed on the plaque.

"That's funny." Caron frowned as she noticed some funny lettering that she'd never seen before. But she was unable to work out what was so strange about it—just that it looked odd.

However, now wasn't the time to linger, as someone else might come by. So quickly glancing over her shoulder one last time, she took hold of the plaque, a paw on both sides. Caron turned it to the left first until she heard a click, then to the right and there was another click.

"Okay. What was it next?" Hoping she had remembered correctly she turned it back to the left for a third click.

At that point, the plate popped away from the base like a door, revealing the hollow inside.

"Yes!" Quickly taking the crown out of her tunic, Caron carefully placed the precious crown inside before closing the plaque. She pulled on it just to make sure it was shut tight. "Phew!"

Turning her head, the Lyon-girl checked once more that no-one was about before memorising the words.

"I must talk to the others about this. It could be an important clue." Before departing their separate ways, they had agreed to meet at Whitesands Bay the next day to think where to go next. Now she had something to tell them.

Caron had problems containing her delight as she walked up the path that would take her home. She skipped along, stopping to pick some rosemary from a bush as she passed by, inhaling the scent. What an exciting first day the Quest had been!

As she went over in her mind all that had happened, she said to herself, "I wonder where the other parts of the crown are?"

CHAPTER SEVEN

The Strange Lettering

Braith was pleased there was no one around on Whitesands Bay when he arrived the next day. It wasn't surprising. Generally, Merfolk stay away from the Lyon-people. It's not that they didn't get on, but they had little in common. His people lived in the sea and Caron's on land. And as for the Fae, they were so mysterious that most Merfolk didn't think they really existed.

He glanced up the beautiful beach. The sand looked so white it glinted silver in the sunlight. Braith chuckled. He knew exactly why. The sand was formed from the tails of Merfolk which turned to silver sprinkles whenever they walked on the land.

As he swam into the shallows, Braith saw Nia peering out from behind a bush and waved at her. Cupping his hands around his mouth, he shouted. "Come on down. There's nobody here."

He enviously watched as Nia skipped down the narrow steps. She made it seem so easy to walk. Braith knew if he thought really hard he could gain legs and walk on the sand like the adult Merfolk. But it was too hard for now.

"Hello," said Nia shyly as she approached the edge of the sea. "Any sign of Caron yet?"

Braith shook his head as he pulled himself up onto the sand. Although he liked the Lyon-girl, he was a tiny bit scared of her still. At least she wasn't as fierce-looking as her father—he was the Lord of Lyon Isle after all! But Nia was easy to like, just a bit shy and quiet.

"Do you think she managed to hide the part of the crown I found?" he asked.

Nia didn't answer, because at that moment the Lyon-girl came running full pelt around the headland and threw herself onto her knees in front of them. A shower of sand flew up and they all jumped back with a laugh.

"Sorry," she giggled.

"Where did you hide the crown yesterday?" asked Braith. He'd wished he could have gone with her.

"In the herb gardens. There is a statue of a lion."

"Oh, I've heard about it," exclaimed Nia, clapping her hands. "The one of the first Lyon-Lord."

Braith wasn't familiar with this statue. So, he asked curiously, "Where exactly did you hide it? On the head of the lion?"

"No, silly!" Caron glanced over her shoulder just to make doubly sure there was no one else around and then leaned toward the other two. In a low voice she said, "If you turn the plaque to the left it moves. There is a sequence you have to do. Left, right, left. And then it opens and there is a gap behind. Just large enough to put the crown inside." She sat back on her heels with a satisfied look on her face.

"Oh! I wish I could have seen that." Braith was pleased that their precious crown was safe. Nia nodded happily.

Caron crossed her legs, then cupping her chin in one paw, she put her elbow on one of her knees and frowned. Braith was curious about what the Lyon-girl was going to say.

"You know, there was something rather strange with that plaque. Oh, it closed all right, but as I was opening it, the words looked peculiar."

"What do you mean? Did the words change as you opened it?" queried Nia, for once contributing to the conversation. Her voice was very sweet and musical. It was mostly just Caron and Braith speaking when there were the three of them.

"No. Not that. Look, let me write the words in the sand and you will see," Caron said.

Braith was intrigued and lay on his stomach in the sand, pushing himself up with his forearms to see what the Lyon-girl was writing.

erecTed on lyon islE to commeMorate its founder Peryn by the Lyon-men, merfoLk and faE 28th May 1342.

The Lyon-girl sat back on her heels, wiping her paws. "I think that's correct."

"What's wrong with that?" Braith asked, unable to see what was so odd.

Nia stood up and moved to stand next to Caron, directly in front of the words. Tilting her head on one said she stated, "I can see what you mean."

Braith grunted. "Well, will someone please show *me*?"

Meanwhile, Caron grabbed Nia. "What is it?" the Lyon-girl asked, her voice indicating her urgency.

"Don't you to see it?"

Caron jiggled Nia's arm, as frustrated as Braith. "Tell us!"

"Some of the words are wrongly capitalised. That's all."

Both Braith and Caron turned back to the words.

"Look there." Nia pointed to the capital T in the word erecTed. "And here." She indicated the E in islE written in the sand.

Caron scuttled backwards causing Nia to hurriedly jump to the side. "Let's write just those letters over here." She then wrote T and an E. "What's next?"

"M," said Nia. "There in commeMorate."

"That's right," cried Braith. "And there's P in Peryn. Although, that's supposed to be a capital letter as it's the first letter of his name. Write it anyway and we can erase it if it's wrong."

Caron swiftly drew these letters in the sand. Then there was a moment's silence while they all searched for more. "Ooo! I can see an L in merfoLk," stated the Lyon-girl.

Nia noticed the last letter, an E in faE.

As she finished writing the last letter, Caron sat back on her heels and all three looked down at the sand.

T E M P L E

"Temple. Does anyone know what that means?" Braith was a little disappointed. He expected some exciting revelation, maybe a spell to make the crown whole or something.

Caron was biting one of her claws. "Maybe it's a clue to where we need to go next. I mean, the crown that Braith found was just one piece. The Quest is to find them all and put them back together."

Braith nodded, but part of him wondered how much of the Quest he could go on if it meant parts were on land. "So, do you know where this temple is, Caron?"

The Lyon-girl shook her head.

"I think I know." They turned to look at Nia, who was trembling with excitement.

"Well?" Braith wished he could get up and shake it out of the Fairy.

"I might be wrong, but there's a stone temple in the woods where the Lyon-Lords used to hold court in the olden days."

Caron jumped to her feet. "Do you know where it is?"

"I—I think so," Nia stammered.

"Well, let's go now!" Caron grabbed Nia's hand and started to run toward the cliff path nearly pulling the fairy off her feet.

They had forgotten about the Merboy and had only gone a few steps when Caron suddenly stopped and jerked around. "Oh, Braith! You can't come."

"Yeah. Tell me about it," he complained. "You guys go. But come back and tell me if you find anything."

Caron walked back and crouched down, placing a paw on Braith's shoulder. "I believe this Quest is going to be a team effort. Nia and I couldn't have gone into the octopus cave. Only you could do that. And Nia didn't go with me to the lion statue. And without Nia we wouldn't have known about the temple. We are a trio of Questers, all in this together. Okay?"

Braith was heartened by Caron's words. "How about we meet by the mill pond same time tomorrow? I can get upstream to there."

They agreed this was a great plan and the two girls ran off, leaving Braith desperately trying to get his legs in case something like this happened again.

CHAPTER EIGHT

The Temple

Nia and Caron were climbing Castle Rock. Nia got to the top first, Fairies being light and quick on their feet. She could hear Caron huffing as she clambered up the hill to join her. Thankfully, Braith wasn't with them as he would have struggled even if he did have legs, however, it felt strange to go somewhere without him. Somehow, they had become a trio even despite only knowing each other a few days.

Although the ruined castle on the rock was fun to explore, it wasn't where they needed to be. But it was a good vantage point. So, while waiting, Nia scanned the woods. The Fairy admitted to herself privately that she wasn't exactly sure where the temple was. She only knew about it from tales and had suggested climbing up this hill as it was very high. Nia thought it might help them spot something that looked like a temple in the distance. Besides which, she was fairly sure it was somewhere near Castle Rock.

Caron came up alongside her, breathing heavily. She slumped on the ground. "Phew!"

Nia smiled.

"So, is this it? It doesn't look much like a temple." Caron stood up to look at the castle ruins.

"No, this isn't it. This is the old castle."

"Why did we come here then?" the other girl grumbled.

"The temple is close by… I think."

Caron turned on Nia. "What do you mean, 'you think'?"

Nia jumped. "W-well, I never said I was certain where it was. From here we can see down into the valley and across to the other side. Let's look hard to see if we can spot anything."

The Lyon-girl huffed, came up behind Nia and patted her on the shoulder. "Good thinking." Caron crouched down onto her haunches, resting her head in her paws.

The two girls were silent as they scanned the woods. Suddenly Nia pointed to something on a nearby hill off to the right. "Look. That might be it." In fact, she was pretty sure now she had found it. Her keen Fairy eyes could see a domed structure peeping through the dense foliage. There weren't any Fae homes around this part of the woods, everything was so overgrown—but it looked like the building she was searching for.

Caron craned her head forward, trying to see where Nia was pointing. "Oh yes. That seems possible. Let's go there now."

Climbing down from Castle Rock was far quicker than going up and they ran over to the other hill, but it was harder than either of them expected because the area was covered in ivy. It took them a while to find the structure they had seen until Nia thought of cutting through the undergrowth instead of going around it.

At Caron's first attempt to slash the thicket of ivy, her paw came into contact with stone. "Ow!"

They made a renewed effort to push through, but the Fairy was too little to break the mass of foliage. *Just as we are nearly there,* Nia thought with a sob.

"Don't worry. I can do that." With her claws, the Lyon-girl managed to hack away at it and soon they cleared enough to enter.

Nia looked at the building they had uncovered—it was round, with a domed roof held up by several stone pillars. She jumped up and down in delight. "Yes! This is it! This is the stone temple!"

Caron slapped the Fairy on the back in her happiness but had to quickly grab her as Nia fell forward with the force of her movement. "Sorry. I forget you aren't as strong as me."

The Fairy smiled. "That's all right. So, we're here. What next?"

They looked at each other, not sure what to do next.

"Will there be another key?" asked Caron.

Nia didn't know. "Maybe the next part of the crown is just here."

"Oh, that's possible," cried the Lyon-girl.

They enthusiastically looked about the structure but before long Nia's smile dropped. There wasn't anything much there. Just a stone bench running around the inside. She sort-of hoped there would be an altar or something with the crown lying on top, except that was far too easy.

Caron was pulling down long swathes of ivy where they descended from the roof, letting more light inside, while Nia searched under the bench.

"Check each nook and cranny," Caron suggested as she started to hack next at the ivy growing around the pillars. "Hmmm."

"What?" asked Nia, jumping up in hope. "Have you found something?"

"Ah, no, sorry. I hoped there would be a clue like some writing or something, like there had been on the wishing tree, but these pillars are just plain."

Nia grunted. "It might not be like last time when there was a key and a chest. The next place the crown is hidden could be a different way of finding it."

The girls slumped to the bench.

As they sat there Nia suddenly spotted something under the bench opposite that she hadn't yet searched. Crossing the space, she flew down onto her knees, reaching as far as her arms could go and eagerly pulled something out from the foliage, coughing at the dust that flew up.

Caron was on her feet behind her. "What have you got?"

"It's an old mat that is all bundled up," stated Nia, slightly disappointed. It was a fairly ordinary piece of carpet, so dirty they couldn't tell what colour it was. As she unfolded it, a glimmer of hope lit within her as she could feel something hard. Something you wouldn't normally find in a mat.

Nia yelped with joy as she pulled the final fold open and held up another piece of the crown.

Caron jumped up and down, "Yes! Yes! Yes!"

The two girls calmed down after a few moments of delight.

"What a shame Braith isn't here," said Caron as she took the crown from the Fairy to look at it.

Meanwhile, Nia went and stood on the mat. "I remember an old Fairy tale about a mat that makes a person vanish and go somewhere else! Maybe we should wish him here."

Caron rolled her eyes. "Don't be silly."

The Fairy giggled. "I can pretend if I want to."

Waving a paw at Nia, the Lyon-girl laughed. "Go ahead. Where would you go if you could? Surely not to the mainland?"

"Goodness, no!" Nia bit her lip. "Where would Braith be now? Maybe somewhere near the sea like the Island of Grifftan." As she spoke these words everything around her started to fade.

CHAPTER NINE

The Disappearing Fairy

Instantly, Nia and the mat disappeared.

Caron gasped and yelled, "Nia! Where are you?!" She rushed forward swiping her paw out in front of her, hoping that Nia was just invisible. But there was nothing there. Caron howled in dismay and clasped her paws over her mouth. "Oh, Nia. What did you do?"

The Lyon-girl was horrified that she had lost her friend when they had only just met and wasn't sure what to do. Should she go and find someone? Her father? Nia's family?

She frowned. "No, not yet. I'm sure there's something I can do here first."

Caron tucked the crown into her tunic as she decided to look around the temple some more, not wanting to admit to her father she had got into trouble just as she was trying to prove she could be of help to him. "Maybe there's another mat that I can stand on and go to the same place Nia went?"

She instantly brightened up thinking that would be a good solution, but then couldn't remember the name of the place Nia had asked the mat to transport her to. Caron stamped her feet in frustration. "Gentle Goddess Friga! I can't remember. Come on, girl—Nia might need you." It suddenly came to her. "Yes! Grifftan! That was it."

Falling to her knees, she hurriedly pulled at the remaining ivy, desperate to find another rug, or material, or anything that would help her get to Nia. Bits of leaves, torn up in her haste, flew up into the air. But Caron couldn't find anything else. There were no more vanishing mats.

The Lyon-girl slumped onto her heels, dropping her head into her paws in despair. Tears started to drop down her face. "Stop it! That won't help Nia." She took a ragged breath as she swiped a paw across her wet face. "Maybe if I stand in the same spot, it will work."

She jumped up and stood where Nia had been and closed her eyes, praying hard that it would work. Speaking slowly and carefully she declared, "I want to go to the Island of Grifftan."

Waiting several seconds, Caron wondered if it had worked as she hadn't felt anything. She opened one eyelid and then both when she saw she was still in the temple. "Oh, Friga!"

Clenching her paws in frustration, the Lyon-girl decided to look around the outside of the temple. This took a while as it was so overgrown, and after a while she stormed back inside thoroughly fed up.

"It was a waste of time coming here. I might have the next part of the crown, but I've lost Nia, and she's been the one with all the knowledge. Well, most of it. And besides which, she's my friend!" Her words echoed around the stone temple.

The Lyon-girl slumped down on the bench and waited, rapidly thinking, should she try to get to Grifftan? Even if she could swim, the current was too fierce, so that wasn't an option.

Some minutes went by. Then a quarter of an hour. Jumping up, she paced around, biting a claw. Should she rush down to Portmer and get one of the fisher-folk to take her over the water to Grifftan? But what happened if Nia wasn't there? And how could she explain what they were doing?

Caron sat down again, jiggling her legs against the bench anxiously. "Come on, Nia. Where are you?"

Then the clock chimed in the distance, and now deeply worried Caron knew she had to do something. Sighing deeply, she started to walk down the steps away from the temple, very disheartened, wondering how she was going to tell Braith the next day. "Forget about Braith. How will I tell Nia's family? Or my father? What sort of Lyon-Lady does that make me, losing one of my team?"

Caron.

The Lyon-girl swiftly twisted around, hoping the Fairy had returned. "Nia?"

But she couldn't see the Fairy. She couldn't see anyone. Caron shook her head. "I must be dreaming." She started to walk down the valley away from the temple, knowing she had to admit everything to her father.

Caron came the voice again.

The Lyon-girl ran back up the hill, emerging into a clearing close to the temple. "Who's that?" Whatever it was, it didn't sound like Nia. Caron's heart started pounding. This was scary. Was it Graham playing tricks on her?

Then a Unicorn appeared from behind the bushes.

"Oh." She stepped back, not expecting that. If she hadn't been so worried about Nia, she might have been more amazed at seeing the mysterious creature that only appeared to the people of the Isle at certain times, warning them of danger, usually. She had only seen it once before, when her father had become Lyon-Lord on the death of her grandfather. She recalled Leolin wondering why the creature had appeared at that time.

Nia will be safe.

"What?" Had it spoken to her? But she hadn't seen its mouth move. "D—did you say something?" She took a tentative step forward.

Go home now. All is well.

The creature was talking inside her mind. She raised a paw to her head. "How do you do that?" Then she realised what the Unicorn had said, and her jaw dropped. "Nia is okay? Really? Oh, thank Friga!"

Caron's legs were shaking in relief. "Where is she then?" She searched around her, hoping to see Nia, but there was no-one else except the creature who stood at the back of the clearing.

Meet with Braith tomorrow as arranged. Nia will come to you.

The Lyon-girl frowned in confusion. "How do you know about Braith? Or Nia, come to that? And how did you know we were due to meet up again?" This was very extraordinary, but the creature had nothing more to say and it melted back into the trees.

"Don't go!" Caron ran to where the animal had been, but there was no sign of it. "Well, that was very strange."

But she felt better now, instinctively knowing she could trust the Unicorn and that Nia was fine.

As she walked out of the woods to put the crown in the secret hiding place in the statue before going home, she contemplated what had happened. If Nia was okay, why hadn't she come back straight away? And why did the Unicorn come to tell her this—a creature who only appeared in times of danger?

CHAPTER TEN

Grifftan

Nia was terrified. Where was Caron? Where was the stone temple? All she could see was mist around her. There was a whooshing noise in her ears and the mat beneath her feet was floating. It was the most terrifying experience of her life—even worse than speaking to a Lyon for the first time.

Suddenly the mist cleared, and Nia landed on the ground with a thump, tumbling forward off the mat.

"Oooof." She landed a few feet away on top of a rock.

As she sat up, pushing her long hair out of her eyes, Nia looked around her and frowned. There was no forest at all.

"Oh, fairydust." Nia froze in fear. Somehow, she had been transported somewhere else. Then she had a moment of realisation. She had pretended it was a magical mat and joked about going to the island of Grifftan. So, was she now there? Swallowing hard, she turned her head to look around and became aware that Lyon Isle was over the water from her.

Yep. There is Portmer with the cliffs and the woods high on the hillside. She could even see the Bell Tower from where she was.

She wasn't worried now, just amazed. "I'll go to the mat and wish myself back at the temple."

But as Nia started to think about returning, she saw mist starting to curl up over the edges of the island she was on and she shivered.

She suddenly remembered that Grifftan was dangerous. If you were on the island when the mist covered it, the island would disappear—and you would be lost forever!

Standing up in a hurry, she rushed back to the mat but lost her footing on the damp grass and slid down the side of the hill. "Ahhh!" As she fell, she tried grabbing hold of the grass…it was too slippery!

Down she went, into a gully. She tried to stop her fall by digging her feet into the ground, but stones slithered away beneath her feet.

Finally, she came to a stop on the precipice—the edge of the cliff. Nia looked over the side. The sheer drop to the sea made her dizzy.

She carefully sat back. "Ouch." She had grazed her arms and legs in the fall. But that was the least of her problems. The question she asked herself now was, "How do I get back up?" What was even more worrying… she could see the mist coming toward her!

Nia wanted to cry but knew it wouldn't help. There was no-one to come to her rescue. No Caron or Braith to help her. She had to be brave by herself.

Blinking back tears, Nia swiftly got to her feet, and with her back hugging the cliff side, she reached out a hand to guide herself. The section of hill she was on seemed to slope upwards. She thought she could get back to the top if she moved very carefully—and very quickly! The mist was only a little way from her feet now.

She was so nervous; her breath was coming rapidly as she climbed higher. More than once, her foot skidded on some loose stones and she yelped in fear. Part of her wanted to just stay where she was, hoping someone would come to her rescue. The other part of her knew it was impossible to wait and she continued as fast as she dared.

Just as she was reaching the top, something stung her.

"Ouch!"

Pulling her hand to her body, Nia could see she had cut herself.

Whatever was that?

Leaning forward, she looked into a crevice. Something shiny was sticking out. "Shimmering fairydust!" she gasped. It was a sword!

Reaching in carefully, Nia took hold of the handle of the sword—she thought it was called a pommel—and pulled it free. It was lighter than it appeared, despite being nearly as long as her body, and very beautiful.

But there wasn't time to admire it as a tendril of mist entwined around her ankle. She yelped and hurriedly scrambled up the last part of the hill, flinging herself and the sword onto the mat.

There was no time to waste. Mist had enveloped nearly all of Grifftan. "Take me to the stone temple. *Now!"*

Haziness surrounded her, and Nia burst into tears, thinking she had left it too late. She would never see her family again. Never see Caron and Braith. And never see the crown in one piece. At that moment in time, she was extremely glad that Caron had been holding the crown when Nia had vanished.

Then, suddenly, she heard another whooshing noise and landed with a thump on a hard floor. The Fairy gasped. She was *back* at the stone temple.

Nia couldn't believe her luck and sobbed her relief. "Oh, thank goodness!"

It was a few moments, though, before she became aware that Caron wasn't there.

"Caron? Caron! Where are you?" It didn't take long before Nia realised she was all alone.

As first the Fairy was really annoyed the Lyon-girl had gone off and left her. But then she frowned; the sun was quite low in the sky. Had she really been gone that long? Maybe time went funny on Grifftan. Was Caron worried about her? She hoped the Lyon-girl hadn't done something silly like try to get a boat across to the little island—particularly as it had probably disappeared by now.

Just as she was wondering what to do next, Nia saw a message etched on the ground in Fairy language. She didn't think Caron had learned Fae already. So, who had left the message? Bending down to read it, she smiled when she saw it said, 'mill pond tomorrow' and recalled the arrangement for the three of them to meet there the next day.

"I have so much to tell them," she whispered as she skipped down the temple steps carrying the sword. "They won't believe it."

CHAPTER ELEVEN

The Sword

"There she is!" Caron cried as Nia came running toward them very early the next day. She ran over to the little Fairy and pulled her into her arms, swinging her around in delight.

Braith was envious that Caron could run over to Nia to hug her. He wished he had legs and could do that. While they'd been waiting for the Fairy to arrive, Caron had been telling him about their adventures at the stone temple. He'd gasped in dismay when the Lyon-girl had told him Nia had wanted to go to the island of Grifftan. So he was relieved to see the Fairy peering around the side of a tree, making sure they were there.

"We thought you had gone forever!" Braith cried out, trying to get her attention. He wanted to know where she had been, as he was pretty sure she never went to the mysterious island.

Caron came to a stop and let Nia down. "I waited at the temple for what felt like hours."

Nia gulped. "But I was only gone for a little while. At least, it seemed such a short time."

The Lyon-girl shook her head. "Nope. You were gone for hours. I was wondering how I was going to tell your family when a Unicorn appeared."

"Yes, and—" Braith started to say. He'd already heard about the creature.

But Caron continued. "It told me you were safe and not to wait for you."

"How can that be?" queried Nia.

"Anyhow, *where were you?"* demanded Braith.

Nia turned to the Merboy who was in the mill pond, leaning his arms on stones that formed a circle around the edge. "The mat really did take me to Grifftan!"

"No way!" Caron was amazed. Braith was so dumbfounded he couldn't speak. He knew how dangerous that island was.

"Yes, way. And look what I found there!"

"You found another piece of the crown?" cried the Lyon-girl in delight raising her paws in the air.

"Unfortunately, no. But something else exciting."

Nia went to get the long satchel she had dropped when Caron had grabbed her. She pulled a sword out. "Ta da!"

How in all the ocean had she found that? Braith thought, feeling rather jealous of the girls who had not only found another part of the crown but now a shiny sword as well.

Nia laid the blade on the stones by Braith and sat down beside it. Caron stepped forward and crouched, reverently caressing the blade of the sword.

"It's beautiful," the Lyon-girl whispered in awe.

Braith couldn't believe how shiny it was. "It's so bright I can hardly tear my eyes away." It was mesmerising.

"Turn it over," requested Caron urgently. "Does it have any markings or words or anything?"

"Why do you ask that?" queried Braith.

The Lyon-girl glanced at him. "The sword could be another clue to where we need to go next!"

Nia gasped and quickly turned it over but to their collective disappointment there was just a pattern around the top, like a plait of rope, but nothing to say who it belonged to or suggesting where they should go next.

"Where exactly did you find it?" asked Caron after a moment's silence while they all thought.

"I fell down a gully and as I was getting back up on to the cliff top, I cut my hand on it."

Braith then asked the question he had been wondering ever since Nia said she had gone to Grifftan. "How did you get away from the mist?" The Merfolk always stayed away from the island.

The Lyon-girl's eyes opened wide. It was clear the implications had just hit her.

Nia jumped to her feet and demonstrated how she had inched up the hill until reaching the top and jumped on the mat just in time.

"You are sooooo lucky. Whatever would I have told everyone if you had been lost on that island!" declared Caron.

The Fairy agreed. "I know. Let's hope we never have to visit there again, I was terrified."

Braith snorted. "So, we now have a sword that doesn't have any clues and a mat that takes us to a disappearing island. And the crown is still incomplete. Let's hope the Humans don't decide to come any time soon!"

The shoulders of all three slumped.

"Could we use the mat to take us someplace else? Hey, we could ask it to take us to the final part of the crown, and then I can go back to sunning myself on the rocks," said Braith with a grin.

The Lyon-girl perked up, but Nia shook her head. "The mat vanished as soon as I got back. I think it is a one-time-only thing."

Caron groaned. "Why did you have to make that silly wish?" When Nia looked like she was going to cry, the Lyon-girl hugged her. "Never mind. If that was the real part of the Quest, then it would have led us to a proper clue. Somewhere we were supposed to go to find another part of the crown."

"Oh, so we are back at the start." Braith huffed in annoyance. The Quest was proving harder than he thought it would.

The Lyon-girl looked serious. "Not really. We have two parts of the crown. I briefly looked at it yesterday as I stashed it away in safety and it looks like we just need one more piece."

Nia clapped her hands excitedly.

Caron continued. "We were meant to go to the stone temple. Remember?" Braith nodded. "The words on the plaque led us to the temple and as the mat was the only thing there other than the crown, one of us was supposed to go to Grifftan and find the sword."

"Well, do either of you know what to do with it?" asked Braith in frustration, looking from one girl to the other.

Nia shrugged and tentatively suggested, "Do you think it would be good to fight off the Humans?"

Braith gave a war cry and flipped his tail in the water splashing Caron. "Yay! That's how we fight them! With this sword. We'll cut them to shreds!!"

The Lyon-girl stood up, shaking the water droplets from her tunic. "Stop it, Braith! That's enough."

"But what use is the crown then?" asked Nia in a quiet voice and both Braith and Caron turned to her in astonishment.

CHAPTER TWELVE
The Mill Pond

Caron dismissed Nia's comment immediately. "The crown has to be useful for something, otherwise there wouldn't be a prophecy. As for the sword..." She it picked up and studied it, testing the sharpness of the tip. "It's really too small to do much damage. It might be big for you guys, but it is more like the size of a dagger to us Lyons."

"Oh, that reminds me—"

The Lyon-girl interrupted Braith. "It's quite sharp, though. I suppose we could use it to jab a Human's hand if they grabbed us." She simulated the action, pretending to stab into the Merboy's.

He quickly pulled his hand away as she laughed. "Or we could—"

Nia interrupted Braith this time. "Or we could stick it up their backsides."

Her mime was even more dramatic, and the two others turned to stare at the little Fairy in astonishment. Caron was more than a little stunned, then she chuckled. "You are more bloodthirsty than I thought a Fairy ever could be. Remind me never to cross you."

Nia looked abashed. "Or we could wave it over the crown and hope it might make it whole."

The Lyon-girl nodded at the Fairy. "That's a much more sensible solution. I'll try it when I get to the other pieces."

"Listen, guys—"

Caron finally turned to the Merboy. "Sorry, Braith, you have a suggestion, too?"

He gave her a look of annoyance before he said what he had been trying to tell them. "While I was waiting for you both to arrive, I noticed something sparkling in this pond, but it is so murky I couldn't see anything, and then I forgot all about it until now."

"Really? Where?" queried the Lyon-girl as she turned to squint at the dark water.

"Over there." Braith gestured to the far side.

Caron sighed sadly. "We won't find anything in here, I reckon. There are too many water lilies and stuff and it's a rather gloomy spot." She glanced around her and there were several trees blocking the light.

The Merboy came up with an idea. "How about using the sword like a stick to feel for anything?"

"What?"

"Well, if it's no good as a sword."

The Lyon-girl gave him an uncertain stare. "I suppose. Although it seems wrong to use it for such a mundane purpose. Where did you say the glinting happened again?"

Braith moved to the spot he had mentioned and swam about, making sure of it. "Yep. Somewhere about here."

Just as Caron went to that side of the pond, a ray of sunlight peeked through the clouds for an instant and she barked in excitement as something glinted. "I can see it!" She rushed over and flung herself face down on the stone edge, reaching into the water with the sword, urgently trying to find the object that had briefly sparkled in the sunshine.

"I can't feel anything." She was rather frustrated.

Nia jumped about behind her while Braith tried diving down. His head burst out of the water. "Nothing," he said in disgust.

Caron edged closer to the water pushing the sword in deeper. Her arm was in the pond up to her shoulder and her tunic was now sopping wet, but she was sure she had seen what Braith had noticed before.

Clunk.

"Oh. I think I've got something, but I can't get a grip on it."

She could hear the other two gasp in anticipation. Finally, the sword hooked around the item she'd felt, and she carefully edged backward pulling it out of the water. They all held their breaths as the sword came above the water.

"Gentle Goddess Friga!"

Then they all fell about laughing. It was an old pail. She flung it onto the grass where it landed with a thump.

"In all the seas, what a thing to throw into the water. Don't people realise junk like this gets washed down the stream into the sea?" cried Braith in disgust. He huffed. "I'm going home."

The Merboy swam toward the end of the pond where the water flowed through a narrow channel which eventually led back to the sea.

"It's getting late and Lyon-people will start travelling about the villages soon, so I'd better get back to the woods. I have lessons today, anyway," said Nia as she trudged away.

"Wait a minute!"

The other two Questers stopped at Caron's frantic cry. She had decided to try just once more and felt something else. It wasn't a clunk this time, more of a tinkle. Cautiously angling the sword between the prongs to pick it up, she raised it above the water. It shone brightly in the soft light. It was the third piece of the crown!!!

"We've done it!" Braith slapped his tailfin on the water again causing a ripple across the pond.

"Careful. I might drop it." Caron slowly lifted the sword carrying the final crown part until she could lay it on the ground next to her. Her arm was trembling.

Nia rushed toward her and flung herself to her knees staring at the crown in awe. "The last piece. Shimmering fairydust!"

Braith dived over to where the girls were sitting staring at their find. Then he noticed something. "Look! There are words on the sword now!"

Caron abandoned the crown and quickly turned the sword, so she could look at the flat side. Sure enough, there was now something written along the length in beautiful old handwriting.

"What does it say?" asked Nia, excitement evident in the tone of her voice.

"I'm not sure." Caron knelt so that the others could see.

Sunlight bounced off the bright metal, blinding them for a moment. Then they all bent their heads to read it.

CUT THE MAGICAL CHAIN

CHAPTER THIRTEEN

The Final Piece of the Crown

Nia read the words, then traded puzzled looks with the other two. "What does *that* mean?"

Braith dropped his forehead onto the stones. "Not again! Just as we work out the other clues, here is *another* puzzle."

"Well," began Caron as she stood up, "I guess if it was easy, anyone could have solved the clues. I've been thinking, it was meant to be that one person from each of our people were supposed to work together to find the crown."

That astonished Nia and made her pleased inside that it was she amongst all the Fae that was doing this Quest.

"Think about it," the Lyon-girl continued. "Neither Nia nor I could have gone into the octopus cave. And I found the words on the lion statue. And Nia knew about the stone temple."

Braith broke into their self-congratulations. "But this is a sword and now it talks about a chain. Is this a different Quest, do you think?"

Nia gasped. She hadn't thought about that.

"Maybe," said Caron, a little uncertain. "But I do know that we have now got another part of the crown. The last part, I think."

Nia had forgotten about the piece that Caron had fished out of the pond, they had all had been so amazed by the words on the sword. She clapped her tiny hands together, her bracelets making a tinkling sound as the Lyon-girl picked up the forgotten crown where it lay by the pond.

Caron handed it to Nia, giving Braith the sword. "You guys stay here with these. I'll run and get the other parts of the crown and we'll try to put it together. The herb garden with the lion statue isn't very far from here."

"Be quick," cried Braith. Nia was also worried Lyons would notice them. The sun was getting higher in the sky.

While he and Nia impatiently waited, they tried to work out what the magic chain could be. "Is there anywhere in the woods that is chained?" queried the Merboy.

Nia shook her head. She couldn't think of any places. There were few buildings in the forest, and they were generally old and ruined. And no trees were ever chained.

"What about in the sea?" she asked back.

"Nah. Any chains would rust in the water."

"But if it's magical, it might not go rusty," the Fairy cleverly stated.

Braith made a face as he thought hard. "There was an old anchor in the cave of the octopus, but it didn't have any chain attached."

Nia's shoulders drooped in disappointment. She was so deep in thought, wracking her brain, she didn't notice Caron's half-brother, Graham, until Braith unexpectedly pushed her off the stones. "Hey!" she cried.

He hissed, "Shh! Hide! Quick!"

She stumbled to her knees as the Merboy dropped back into the water with a plop. The Fairy stood up, wondering what game Braith was playing. Then she heard voices. Nia anxiously looked around her for somewhere to hide, then froze as she couldn't think what to do.

"I'm sure I saw Caron run down this way." She could hear Graham's voice coming closer. Desperation surged through Nia and she dived into a nearby bush in a panic.

Just in time. She could hear the heavy footsteps of several Lyons as they strode by her hiding place, their clothes brushing her hiding place as they passed, and she froze.

"Maybe she went to the shops. She's already in trouble for going out so early and not doing her chores."

One of his friends chuckled. "I bet you are only mad because you had to do them instead!"

Graham must have hit out at his friend because Nia heard the other boy yelp. Then the voices got quieter as they moved away. She stayed where she was, trembling at the close encounter.

"Nia?" whispered Braith. "Where are you?"

The Fairy struggled out of the shrub with some difficulty. "I'm here." She was annoyed with herself. Out of all the places she could hide, she went and chose a rosebush!

Just then Caron came hurrying back. She was out of breath, having run all the way to the herb garden and back. The Lyon-girl flopped down onto the stone rim of the pond, and opening her tunic, she brought out the other two pieces of the crown. "I had to go the long way round as I saw Graham from a distance. He didn't see me, thankfully, but thought I'd better keep them hidden in case I bumped into anyone else."

"Yes. He came this way!" snorted Braith in disgust.

"Oh, Friga. Did he see you?"

Nia shook her head. "No, but I heard him say you were in trouble."

Caron snorted. "He's always making things difficult for me. I'll deal with it when I get home."

Nia rubbed her bare arms where the thorns of the rose bush had scratched her as she glanced anxiously over her shoulder. She didn't like Caron's half-brother. There was no one there now, so she turned back to look at the three pieces of the crown.

"Okay. It's safe now but let's do this quickly. Look!" said Caron excitedly. "I noticed before that these two fit like this, I think." As she joined the first two pieces together, Nia heard a click as they neatly fit into place.

The Fairy clapped her hands in glee.

Braith picked up the other piece and copying how Caron had fitted the other two pieces, he attempted to do the same with the third part, but his wet hands were slippery and the crown fell towards the pond.

As they all gasped, Nia quickly put her hands out to catch the crown, nearly dropping it herself. "Gosh, it's heavy."

"Look, I'll hold the first two pieces while you, Nia, take the last part and, Braith, you click it into place," said Caron.

With the three of them working together, they soon had it completed and found it was a complete circlet. They had finished the Quest!

Or had they? Nia noticed there was a gap at the front, encircled by lots of small jewels. "What do you think that's for?"

CHAPTER FOURTEEN

Merschool

"Fifty dolphins plus twenty shells plus six starfish. Can you work out the sum? That includes you, Braith!"

Braith jerked up from where he was slouching against the wall in the Mer-school. He really wasn't interested in mathematics. What he wanted was to be out hunting down lost crowns and magical chains with Caron and Nia. The only good thing was that he knew both the girls were also in school that day, so he wasn't missing out by not being there.

It was now several days after they had found the last piece of the crown. After the excitement of putting it together, they had been extremely disappointed to find there was still a bit missing.

A sea urchin came flying in his direction, much to Braith's irritation. It had clearly been thrown by the two giggling Merchildren near the front of the class.

"Since none of you are really interested in sums today," the teacher began, drawing Braith's attention back to the class, "I will tell you a story that will make you realise how important sums are."

There was a shuffling amongst Braith's fellow school pupils as they all put down their slates and chalks to listen to the teacher.

"This is the story of the lost crown of Lyon Isle."

Braith's eyes nearly bulged out of his head as the teacher calmly stated the nature of the story. *How did he know what we've been up to?* Braith warily glanced around the other Merchildren, just to see what their reaction was, then he slowly gave a side glance at the teacher just in case he was looking in Braith's direction and gave a silent sigh of relief when there was no attention on him. He was intrigued to hear what the teacher was about to tell them.

"After fleeing from the Humans and landing on this island, the crown—which is said to have magical properties—was broken into three pieces and each piece given to one of the island's peoples. One piece went to see Merfolk who hid it somewhere safe. I am not telling you where, but Mercouncil know where it is."

Braith bit his lip. *Uh oh.* He now knew why it was in the octopus cave. *It's not there anymore.*

He was beginning to feel so guilty at what he and the girls had done, that he nearly missed what the teacher was saying next. "The second piece went to the Fae—we have no idea where they hid theirs. Somewhere equally safe, I imagine."

Braith backed into the shadows trying to hide himself from the teacher, knowing the second piece was probably the one Nia found in the stone temple in the woods. He knew exactly where the last piece was!

"And the final section was kept by the Lyon-Lord at the time and it is likely that they hid it somewhere in one of their buildings."

The Merboy goggled. He really wanted to tell the teacher they had found it in a pond in the midst of the Lyon villages, but kept his mouth shut.

"However, the point is that there are three pieces to the crown to represent each of the species who live here."

Braith frowned. There was a fourth piece, surely? He alone amongst everyone in the cave knew that there was a hole for another bit. Then the teacher dropped a bombshell.

"And in the very centre of the crown there is a gap for a jewel—a giant emerald."

Gasping aloud along with everyone else, Braith's mind was buzzing. More than ever, he wanted to get out and tell Caron and Nia.

Then, one of the others asked a very important question and Braith nearly pinched himself, knowing he should've asked this. "And where is the jewel now, sir?"

"Ah. Now that is something no one can tell you, for it was the Unicorns that hid the jewel but hardly any of this species survive anymore and are very rarely seen."

"What happens when all pieces are all put back together?" asked Braith with great interest.

"Decided to wake up have you, young man? "Braith went a little red-faced as everyone turned to look at him. Thankfully the teacher continued, "It is said, when the crown is in one piece again, it will defeat the Humans once more—but I have no idea how a crown can do that, and I am rather suspicious that it is nothing more than a tale to tell children. Now, back to the lesson. How many peoples do we have on this island?"

"Four," piped up the Mergirl sitting in front of Braith.

"Wherever do you get four from? Didn't I tell you there were three pieces to the crown."

The girl stuttered and Braith felt sorry for her. "Th-there were the Lyon-men, the Merfolk, the Fae, and the Unicorns."

Braith nearly giggled at the expression on the teacher's face.

"Hmmm. I should have said 'speaking people' as the Unicorns, despite being intelligent, do not have voices. Okay. That's all for today."

Except one of them spoke to Caron in her mind! But Braith didn't like to contradict the teacher so he didn't say anything.

Desperate to get out, he was the first into the water and rushed to the waterfall where they first met, leaving a simple message in Fae that Nia had taught them, saying he needed to see them.

Unfortunately, he had to wait two more days for the others to arrive and was very agitated by the time they turned up.

"Wherever have you been? I've been waiting for days. I've got something *really* exciting to tell you."

Nia settled onto a stone, her hands clasped in her lap while Caron stood legs apart as she crossed her arms. "We should really be looking for more parts of the crown instead of hearing your stories," said the Lyon-girl.

"But this IS about the crown!"

For once he had their attention. But he was so desperate to tell them that he couldn't wait any longer blurting out, "The missing piece is a giant emerald!"

CHAPTER FIFTEEN

The Jewel in the Crown

Caron frowned at Braith. "How do you know that?" she growled at him, wondering if he was pulling one of his tricks.

"I found it out in school. The teacher didn't realise what we've been doing and told us the story of how each of our people took a part of the crown and hid it. I nearly wet myself at first thinking he knew what we'd been up to."

"You didn't, did you?" Nia giggled.

"Nah."

"How do Merfolk...? No, never mind." Caron waved a paw at him as she thought through what Braith had just told her. "A giant emerald. Well, that makes sense. But I don't know of any."

"But listen," cried Braith. "I haven't told you the *really* important bit. The Unicorns took the emerald!"

Caron sat down with a jolt on the bank, stunned at what the Merboy was telling them.

The grin on his face fell. "But no one knows where it is. Or rather the Unicorns might but we can't speak to them even if we could find them."

She rolled her eyes. "Well, that's not very helpful, then, is it?"

The Merboy grunted. "It's more than you knew."

Nia spoke up. "At least we know what to look for."

"See!"

"All right. It was a good bit of information," conceded Caron. "Does anyone have ideas? Have either of you seen or heard about a giant emerald?"

The three children talked for a bit. But none of them knew anything about this jewel and, unfortunately, the Unicorns didn't have a home like the Lyons, the Fae and the Merfolk. They appeared all over the island but were so mysterious no-one knew for sure where to go looking for them.

Caron frowned "I could go back to the stone temple. That's where the Unicorn came to me before. And it spoke in my mind, so it might tell me where to find the emerald if I return." She jumped to her feet ready to run off back to the temple.

"I've never heard of it being seen at the same place twice," pointed out Nia, much to Caron's frustration.

Braith slapped the water. "So how do we find it, then?!"

Nia shrugged her shoulders. Finally, they decided to go to their own parts of the Isle and think some more. As Caron had to go to the Pantheon that evening for a spring ceremony for the Goddess, she scurried off back up the hill.

****

Caron was late when she finally arrived at the domed Pantheon, which stood high on the cliffs. She tried to sneak in at the back, but her father saw her and frowned in her direction. He nodded his head to indicate she was to stay where she was as the ceremony had already started.

Help me, Friga. I'm going to be in trouble later.

She tried to make herself small at the back so that people didn't notice her. Normally she was expected to be on the front benches, but for once she could watch as her parents performed the rites to honour the Goddess. Despite Graham taking pride of place at the front of the procession, she found it to be a beautiful ceremony. and began to relax, smiling at how beautiful her mother looked in a flowing silver cape over her red dress.

Glancing over Tegwen's head, Caron realised she was viewing the building from a different angle to normal and nearly shot to her feet as her eyes came to rest on a picture on the wall above the altar. It showed a Lyon-Lord with a crown on his head!

Caron had never noticed that painting before as she usually sat with her back to it. She stuffed her paw in her mouth to stop herself from shouting out in glee when she saw that the crown was complete *including the emerald*! Caron knew she really needed to look at that picture in closer detail, but how could she do that with everyone around?

Growling softly with frustration, she fidgeted impatiently until the ceremony finished and people started to make their way out. The only problem was Caron would be expected to go home with her parents.

"Caron, come here," boomed her father's voice.

She hurried toward him, looking down, not wanting to see the disapproval in his face.

"Since you were late, you can stay and snuff all the candles out and clean the candlesticks. That is your punishment."

Caron had to fight hard to stop jumping around in excitement. Okay, so there were lots of candles. But it meant she would be alone with the picture. "Yes, of course, Father."

As Leolin narrowed his eyes at her, Caron pretended to be fed up with the task. She didn't really like fooling her parents that way, but it was for a good cause in the end. Her father grunted, and giving his arm to his wife, he led her out of the building.

Graham came up behind Caron making her jump. "You might be home in time for dinner. But I doubt it," he sneered.

"As if I care," Caron jeered at her brother.

She anxiously waited a few minutes for everyone to depart, then, turning swiftly, she hurriedly pulled over a chair to get closer to the painting. It was entitled 'CORAL CAVE'. The Lyon-Lord was standing in front of a cave that was so red it looked like it was encrusted with jewels.

Standing on either side of the Lyon in the picture were a Fairy and a Mermaid. All of them seemed to be important people, wearing elegant capes. It reminded Caron what Braith had said about their peoples working together.

"What about the Unicorn?" Her voice echoed around the huge room, startling Caron as she thought someone else was there.

Giggling a little to herself, she looked at the picture again and suddenly noticed a Unicorn was standing in the shadows just inside the cave entrance.

"Oh," she said excitedly. "We really need to find this place."

But it was too late to go back to Nia and Braith. It would have to wait for the next day. Then she huffed, remembering she still had to deal with the candles. At least they knew where to hunt for the jewel now!

CHAPTER SIXTEEN

Cove Shore

Nia ran down the hill toward the beach the day after Braith had delivered his exciting news. This was the next bay around the headland to Whitesands. When she'd seen Caron's message in the usual place with the words 'Cove Shore', Nia had wondered why Caron had asked them to this particular beach.

She waved as she saw Braith already waiting.

"Hey, you two!" Caron yelled as she came charging up the beach from another direction.

The three of them met at the shoreline, Braith pulling himself up on to the sand. It wasn't an easy part of the Isle to get to as it was far from anywhere and Nia found she'd had to walk a long way around to avoid going through the dreaded *Wild Woods* that no Fae ever entered.

Braith noticed Caron had the sword tucked in a sheath attached to her belt as she approached. "Why are you wearing the sword? Is that the exciting news you wanted to tell us?"

"I know where we have to go next! We might need the sword. And, in case we do find the emerald, I've brought the crown, too." Caron turned, and they could see she had a bag slung on her back—a knapsack.

Nia glanced excitedly at the Merboy. It felt like they were nearing the end of their Quest. Only what did they do then? No Humans came to Lyon Isle. It was supposed to be secret, so when would anyone need to wear the crown?

"Well?" demanded Braith, showing his impatience. "Why did we have to come here?"

Caron laughed. "Okay, keep your tail on! I saw a clue to the jewel in a picture in the Pantheon. That's the big domed building in the midst of the Lyon villages."

"Oh yes, even I can see that from the sea. But how did a picture tell you where the emerald is?" Braith looked at Nia with a puzzled expression.

"Ah. It showed the rulers of *each* of our peoples including the Unicorns in front of a cave and the title said, 'Coral Cave'. And since I know there are caves hereabouts, that's why I suggested we meet at this place."

There was silence. Then Nia stammered, "W-which one is Coral Cave? There are lots of caves." In fact, this part of the Isle was inundated with coves—lots of recesses in the cliff-side, some of which became caves.

"Oh." The Lyon-girl looked crestfallen. "I hoped Braith might know since the Merfolk live in lots of the coves."

They both turned to look at the Merboy who stared intently back at them, thinking hard. He chewed his hair as he thought. "Well, there are some caves further up the beach which are covered in coral. But can't say I've ever seen a jewel in them."

"Hmm," said Caron, sitting with her head in her paws.

"It can't be that easy, otherwise anyone would have found it before now," stated Nia.

The other two both sighed dejectedly.

She continued, "So maybe we need to look for a hidden cave or something like that."

Caron jumped to her feet. "Yes. If there is coral in the caves you mentioned, Braith, maybe it is in that vicinity. Show us."

Braith rolled back into the sea until he could swim again. He raised an arm for them to follow him up the beach for a bit until they came to a section where the sea came up close to the cliffs. Braith was waiting for them. "I'll look at the caves where the sea enters, and you look at the ones along the sand."

They all went off in search of the cave. The first one Nia went into was very small and had nothing inside apart from a crab who scuttled away as soon as she entered, causing the Fairy to jump out of the way with a tiny screech.

"Not this one," she shouted.

"Nor this," said Caron from the next cave.

"Nothing," yelled Braith, the faintness of his voice indicating he was further away.

Nia went to another cave and immediately stepped back. It was very deep and dark.

The Lyon-girl came up beside her and patted her reassuringly on her shoulder. "I'll go in there. You do the other one."

Gratefully the Fairy ran to the next. She thought she had found something when she saw a rock over a hole, but when she pulled it, it easily fell to one side, however, there was nothing there except more crabs.

It took them some time to investigate all the caves before they met up again, exhausted and hungry even though it wasn't midday yet.

"There was nothing in any of the ones I looked at," said Caron, very frustrated. "What about you two?"

They shook their heads, all wondering where to go next.

Nia looked about the cliff-side and noticed a stream coming from a cove none of them had been in. "Is there anything there?"

"Oh. I haven't tried that one yet," declared Braith. It was the last cove on this beach. Nia and Caron followed Braith as he swam up the stream toward it. There was enough land next to the stream for them to walk, although they had to be careful not to fall in.

To their delight the stream ended at a cave—and it was blocked by a rock.

"What a minute," said Caron. "What's that mark? Sort of like a star." She put her paw over the place.

Nia stared where Caron indicated. The symbol had five points radiating out like a starfish. "It is sort of indented, like you can put something in it."

The Lyon-girl bit a claw. "It's not going to be a key. Totally the wrong shape. What else could go there?"

"I KNOW!"

Nia jumped at Braith's shout and nearly fell in the stream. She was saved by Caron who grabbed her just in time.

"There is a *shell* in my grandmother's collection that fits that shape exactly. Wait for me and I'll get it!"

CHAPTER SEVENTEEN

The Shell

"Braith! Where are you going?"

The Merboy stopped dead still as he swam into his grandmother's bedroom, deep in a group of caves in the cliff-side only accessible from the sea.

Now he was there, Braith wasn't sure how to ask her for a shell from her prized collection.

"Hi, Grandmaid."

Delyth, the Queen of the Merfolk, was lounging on a smooth rock in the corner of her cave. It was easy to see her as the cave was lit up by lightning starfish.

She slapped her tail in the water, making Braith jump. That was a sign that she wasn't happy.

"Come here."

Her voice brooked no refusal and Braith swam over to her, trying to work out what to say.

Delyth sat forward, and reaching out, she raised his chin with one hand as she looked intently into his eyes. She frowned. "Where have you been lately, young man? You are usually getting up to mischief, but I've neither seen nor heard you for a week or so."

"A-around and about," he stammered. "I like exploring and finding things." Well, that was the truth, but he didn't really want to tell her about the Quest. Not yet, anyway, until they had found the emerald.

She grunted and released his chin. "Have you tried getting your legs yet?"

Braith grimaced. He was used to his grandmother's way of changing the subject to catch him out. "They just won't come."

Delyth smiled gently. "Keep trying, my love. They will come when you need them the most. Now, I am off to Mercouncil. Sometimes I have very boring things to do. You are so lucky you won't be King of the Merfolk!"

He giggled at his grandmother's joke as he watched her depart, wondering what it would be like if he had been King. "Nah! Too much like hard work." Thankfully, that responsibility would go to his sister one day as it always went to the women of the Merfolk. There had never been a Merking.

Then he realised he hadn't asked her for the shell. "In all the seas. You squib!"

He groaned and went over to a ledge where his grandmother kept her collection of shells. He knew it was wrong of him to just take it, but she wouldn't be back until nightfall and Caron and Nia would be stuck by the cave all that time. "I'll bring it back later," he said out loud, as if that would make it all right.

Unfortunately, it was too high up. "Not again!" he huffed in exasperation. Braith knew if he had his legs he would be able to climb up the rocks to reach the ledge. But, try as he as he might, his legs wouldn't come.

Braith slumped down in exhaustion. After a moment he decided on a different tactic and pulled himself onto the first rock. He was able to do this as his upper arms were very strong. After giving himself a second to recover from that exertion, he reached up to heave his body onto the next rock. It was like a Merfolk-stair. Then up to the highest boulder.

Success!

From there he was able to get the shell, pushing the other items on the shelf to hide the gap. He felt slightly guilty, but this was important.

"Now, back to the others."

* * * *

Braith held the shell high in one hand to show the others as he arrived back at Cove Shore. He quickly swam upstream to where they were waiting.

Nia clapped her hands in excitement when he handed the shell to Caron. It seemed natural to give it to the Lyon-girl. Even though he wouldn't have been able to reach the indentation without his legs, Caron was their leader. The Merboy didn't mind at all as the Lyon-girl was good at that, whilst Nia was the clever one who knew everything. His job was finding objects.

He watched anxiously as she held the shell over the place in the rock, hoping it was the correct one after all.

It fitted in the recess perfectly!

"I knew it!" Braith slapped his tailfin in the water, pleased with himself.

All three stood back and waited, expecting something exciting to happen—and then nothing!

"What's supposed to happen?" he pondered. "I thought the rock would disappear or something."

"Hmm," said the Lyon-girl thoughtfully. "It must do something. The picture told us to come here and the indentation fits Braith's shell exactly."

"And it's the last cave," declared Nia.

"I could try hitting it with the sword," Caron suggested.

Braith didn't really want her to do that, as it might break his grandmother's precious shell and he had to get it back to her before she noticed it was missing.

When he told her this, Caron rolled her eyes at him. "You shouldn't have taken it without permission."

He huffed. "I know."

"Actually, that's not a totally bad idea." They both looked at the Fairy. "Try hitting it with your paw or pressing hard on it."

Braith grimaced but when Caron carefully pushed it with her big paw, the shell went further back into the cliff with a judder.

"Gentle Goddess Friga."

Then, as the Lyon-girl stood back, they heard a deep groaning coming from the cliff, a grinding noise, and they all jumped away, fearful that the hillside was going to crash down on them.

Instead, the rock covering the cave very slowly rolled a bit and stopped. There was a very narrow gap!

With a yell, Caron ran forward and curled her claws around the space to use her strength to try to force it open further. "Ooof." She tried again but it didn't budge an inch.

"Try pressing the shell in and holding it this time." Braith wasn't sure why he suggested that. It seemed to be the right thing.

The Lyon-girl went back to the shell and tried just that.

There was a long rumble and this time the rock continued rolling until the entrance was totally uncovered. Braith gave a huge sigh of relief when the shell popped out, having done its work.

As the stream rushed through the opening, Braith slid forward with a yelp. Thankfully Caron grabbed his arm, stopping him being sucked inside until the rush of water subsided.

The three children peered into the cave. It was a long, narrow passageway.

Braith whispered in awe as their eyes got used to the darkness, "Look, it's covered in coral." He was unable to believe their luck. Would there also be an emerald as well?

CHAPTER EIGHTEEN

Coral Cave

The three of them moved into the cave, Braith swimming up a stream that now ran through the middle, Nia carefully making her way along a narrow path of sand on one side, whilst Caron took the other track.

"It's very shiny in here," declared Nia.

Braith nodded. "Very red, too."

"Yep. That will be the coral," stated the Lyon-girl. "We are looking for the emerald which will be green, of course."

The three friends looked about for a while.

"I can't see anything," said Caron, frustrated. She thought she would notice it immediately.

"Look there!"

Caron turned in the direction Nia pointed, and up toward the ceiling she could see the emerald in the rock face. But there was no way she could reach it!

Braith spoke. "Why don't you kneel, Caron, and let Nia climb on your shoulders? Can she reach it then?"

As Caron carefully stood up with Nia in place, she realised it was impossible to lift her head to see. "Tell me how far over I have to go, Braith."

She heard a splash behind her as Braith came closer. "Move toward your left by a minnow."

This was a small fish and Caron understood how much she had to move.

"Nia, can you reach out without falling?" asked the Merboy. When it was clear the Fairy wasn't close enough, he added, "Caron, step forward until you are flat against the cave wall.

There was a moment's silence as Nia jiggled about, trying to dislodge the jewel. Caron held tightly onto the Fairy's legs.

"It's not working!"

"Try using the sword to prise it out," suggested Braith.

Nia carefully reached down to take the sword from Caron. She wobbled a bit as they did this, and Caron gripped the Fairy's legs more tightly. "Careful!"

The Lyon-girl heard Nia grunting as she used the sword to dig into the rock.

Then finally some coral fell to the ground and Nia cried in delight. "I've got it!"

Caron had to keep from jumping up and down in delight. Instead, she quickly knelt to let the Fairy down and they crowded around to look at the beautiful jewel now cradled in Nia's hands.

She patted her two friends on their shoulders and grinned at them. "That was great teamwork, Questers!"

Nia smiled broadly and Braith threw a fist in the air.

"Now to put it in the crown." Caron quickly shrugged off the knapsack. Her paws were trembling as she retrieved the crown. "Okay. Here goes." As the other two watched, she carefully used her claws to widen four little prongs that looked as if they would hold the emerald in place in the oval gap. "Give me the jewel, Nia." It fitted beautifully. The Lyon-girl swiftly pressed the wires down so that the emerald was held fast. It was complete!

The Fairy clapped her hands while Caron yelled her triumph and Braith splashed around excitedly.

Then all three started to calm down. They finally had the crown!

"So, what happens next?" asked Nia in a quiet voice. "Do we have to go to the mainland with it to defeat the Humans?"

It was a good question and none of them knew the answer.

Then Nia squealed as the sea started trickling into the cave over the sand to their feet.

"The tide is coming in! It comes in fast here. Quick, you need to get out." Clutching his grandmother's shell, the Merboy swam back to the entrance of the cave.

However, Caron and Nia couldn't make it. The water was rising too fast. Nia screamed and ran further up into the cave.

"Braith, we can't go that way. The sea is coming in too quickly. Will the whole cave fill with water?" the Lyon-girl asked anxiously.

"There has been a rock over the entrance for decades, so I don't know," he answered anxiously.

They soon found out as the water continued to rush in.

"Caron, quick. Here is a way out." The Lyon-girl sloshed through the water to see where Nia was pointing.

Cupping her mouth, Caron shouted down the length of the tunnel, "We will go this way, Braith. You'd better get out while you can."

Placing the crown back in the bag, the Lyon-girl lifted the Fairy up onto a boulder and watched as Nia scrambled out, relieved when she saw the Fairy was safe.

The question was…could she get out as well?

"Come on, Caron. The hole is bigger than it seems."

Moving onto the boulder, Caron, stood up but wasn't sure how to get further. Looking behind her at the water, she took off the knapsack and sword to pass them through the hole to Nia, but the Fairy seemed to have disappeared.

"Nia? Where have you gone?"

"I'm here." The other girl came back, panting heavily. She dropped a vine down the hole, then took the items Caron handed up to her.

"Good girl." Using that, Caron was able to pull herself out and onto the cliff-top.

"Phew, that was close."

Taking back the sword and knapsack, Caron said, "We'd better go home, I guess. I suppose I should give these to my father."

"Well, that was who we were finding them for," said Nia softly, as reluctant as Caron to hand them over.

And what would father do with them, the Lyon-girl wondered as she and Nia walked along the cliff path to go back to their respective homes. She was sad that the Quest was over. It had been fun working with Nia and Braith and going on their adventures, even if sometimes horrifying things had happened, like Nia vanishing on the mat and Braith being caught by the octopus.

Then she started to hum a happier tune, wondering how pleased her father would be when they gave him the crown.

Well done, Caron.

"What? Who was that?" the Lyon-girl cried. "I thought I heard the Unicorn!"

There was a rustling in the trees but neither girl could see anything. "Maybe it was just the wind," said Nia.

Caron wasn't so sure and glanced over the top of the cliff at a place called look-out point. She could see Braith swimming back home and wished she'd had a chance to say goodbye before they scrambled out of the cave. She had envisaged all three of them going to the Lyon villages, or at least, Portmer, and passing the crown to her father in some sort of magnificent ceremony.

But then she looked beyond the Merboy and gasped in horror.

There were ships. Lots of them. And they weren't Lyon ships!!

PART TWO:

The Humans Are Coming!

CHAPTER ONE

The Wild Woods

Nia glanced to where Caron was pointing and was horrified by what she saw on the sea.

"Oh, fairydust. Are those *Human* ships?" Unlike the colourful triangular sails of Lyon ships, these had thick black square sails…and they were *much* larger!

As Caron tried to attract Braith's attention, the Fairy hurriedly counted, "Five, ten, twenty—" There were too many!

The Lyon-girl grabbed Nia's arm and pointed. "That's a relief! He's seen the ships. Look, we have to get back to our peoples to warn them. Braith will go to his. I'm going along the coastal path back to the Lyon villages. Can you go into the forest to your home?"

Nia nodded, but hesitated a moment as the other girl bounded off down the path. There was problem—the quickest way back was through the *Wild Woods*, and she knew that was extremely dangerous.

"I've got to do it," she whispered to herself.

As Nia quickly ran through the nearest section of forest, her heart was bursting—partly from fear of the Humans and partly from the dread of going through the *Wild Woods*. Most of the trees on the Isle were kind-natured—the Fae believed that trees were the spirits of the dead—but these woods were inhabited by evil ones.

She slowed as she approached them, trying to stop herself breathing so hard. Nia thought if she went carefully and silently, she might get through.

It was very dark inside and she had to be careful to avoid landing on twigs or fallen leaves in case they crackled and alerted the spirits. What she could see were huge black trees, with twisted, gnarled trunks and lots of low branches.

Every step she took Nia grimaced when she heard a rustled and glanced around warily, eyeing the closest trees with trepidation. Then she saw another problem. The trees were too thick. There was no way through!

Oh no! What shall I do? she cried to herself. Standing still she started to bite a thumb nail while she looked around her. It felt like the trees were getting closer, and she knew she had to get out of there quickly! She wished Caron was there with her as the Lyon-girl wouldn't be scared. Or even Braith, if only he had his legs, as she knew he would find a way out, somehow.

Making a decision, Nia decided to crawl under the low branches of the tree ahead of her. Carefully kneeling on the ground on all fours, she crept forward one knee at a time, then onto her stomach as she attempted to wriggle past the lowest branch.

Just as Nia thought she was clear and was about to stand up, a wind rustled through the copse of trees, and all the leaves swirled about. Suddenly something clamped onto her ankle!

She looked around. It was a branch of the tree.

"Oh, no!"

Nia jiggled her leg trying to dislodge the branch, and then pulled harder. As she struggled to free herself, another branch slithered out to grab her thigh, then a third took hold of her arm.

She was trapped!

Nia tried to scream for help but in her fright all that came out her lungs was a soft cry that she knew no one could hear...

As she started to sob at her plight, fearful she would never see anyone again—let alone warn the people of the Humans—she heard a loud, echoing bark.

She now had another problem. A giant dog skidded to a stop in front of her. Nia's eyes opened wide in fear and she started to pull back into the trees!

What's worse? The trees or the dog? she thought.

The hound reached out a paw for Nia and she flinched. But instead of clawing her as she expected, he hit the branch holding her!

There was a loud crack as it broke. It freed Nia's arm!

"Thank you. Oh, thank you!" she cried, and with both arms free, she pounded at the remaining branches as the dog took one thick stem in his enormous jaws and shook it about until it released Nia's leg.

Yes! Just one to go. As the dog moved toward the final branch, it suddenly let her go. The dog howled in victory. She was safe!

Nia clapped her hands over her ears, but she was smiling.

"Thank you so much for helping me." She tentatively reached out to pet the dog on the head. In return he licked her hand.

It felt yucky, but she knew instinctively he meant it kindly.

The Fairy then looked about her. They still had to get out of the woods. There was still a possibility they could be trapped again.

Just as she thought this, the trees started to edge closer again and Nia skittered backwards with a squeal.

The giant dog went down on his stomach in front of her.

"Do you want me to climb on your back?" Nia queried with a frown.

He gave a yip which she took to mean 'yes'.

She had never done anything like that before—but if she could become friends with a Lyon-girl and a Merboy, then she could certainly ride a giant dog.

The problem was there was nothing to hold on to, so she grabbed his fur firmly in her hands.

"Sorry, but I have to do this."

The dog didn't seem to mind and as soon as Nia was settled he set off running so quickly Nia closed her eyes in alarm! Holding onto his fur with her hands, she gripped tightly with her legs as he swerved around trees. The Fairy jostled from side to side but somehow managed to stay on top of him, however, when he jumped over a branch she yelped in fear, tumbling forward as the hound landed. She saved herself from falling off only by flinging her arms around his neck.

Thankfully, it was only a short ride before the dog began to slow down. Nia looked around her. They were out of the *Wild Woods* and at the entrance to her part of the forest.

She slid off the dog when he stopped and threw her arms around him.

"You are a saviour."

The dog gave a loud bark before sitting back as if he was waiting.

"Nia. What is that?"

The Fairy twirled around and saw her Uncle Rees. The ruler of her people was standing nearby with some other Fae. They were looking in astonishment at her and the hound.

She rushed over to him. "Quick! We must warn everyone! The Humans are coming!!"

CHAPTER TWO
The Coastal Path

Caron ran quickly along the coastal path, worried how quickly the enemy ships would get to Portmer. Maybe she should have cut through the woods, but Nia's home was in a different part of the forest and she might have got lost without the Fairy. The Lyon-girl was also anxious for both Braith and Nia.

A sound alerted her—like stones rolling down the cliffs. She frowned. There had to be something there for that to happen. Her stomach started knotting. She hoped the Humans hadn't landed already.

The Lyon-girl twisted around, searching the path and trees, unable to see anything.

Then another noise, a grunt, heavy breathing, some cursing!

Caron ran over to the edge and looked down, horrified by what she saw. The enemies were climbing the cliffs! Lots of them! She gasped.

"Oh, no! We are too late. They have come already!"

The Lyon-girl hesitated just a moment. If their ancient enemy had found them, then it was vital to get the crown to her father. The prophecy stated the Humans would only be defeated when the Lyon-Lord wore the crown. And Leolin was on the other side of the island!

There was also something equally urgent—the islanders needed to be warned! Caron made a decision and started running along the path even faster. "If I can get to the lighthouse, maybe that will warn everyone." She wasn't far from that building as she has been running full pelt along the path from the look-out point, so it seemed the best option.

Making sure the knapsack holding the precious crown was firm, Caron sprinted as fast as she could, the sword clanging against her hip. She was mightily glad she had it now, as it could come in useful, after all.

Behind her came shouts—they had reached the top and were chasing her!

Quick! Just one more corner and she was there.

"Get her!" yelled one in a coarse voice, and she ran for her life, her chest heaving with exertion.

Caron was within touching distance of the lighthouse, where she hoped to barricade herself inside, when one of the Humans suddenly came up behind her and grabbed at her bag, pulling a strap off one shoulder.

The Lyon-girl was jerked back, nearly losing the bag with the crown in it!

NO!

However, the Human didn't reckon on the determination of the young Lyon, and Caron slashed out with her claws, slicing his hand.

He let go with a yelp and Caron staggered, pleased to be free, but then more disaster came, as she skidded on some loose stones. Stumbling, she was unable to get her footing, and fell over the edge!

"Oh, FRRRRRRIIIIGGGGAAA!" The Lyon-girl plummeted toward the rough sea. Covering her head in fear, she curled her body into a ball and landed in the water with a huge splash, like a cannon ball!

Oooooofff! That hurt.

But there was a worse problem. Caron had fallen so fast she sank deeply into the water and then she remembered she couldn't swim!

Kicking her legs rapidly the Lyon-girl tried to swim up. Her chest was hurting and she needed to breathe!

No! Please don't let me die now. I must warn my people.

Then something tickled her outstretched paw and she drew it back against her body.

She started to yelp as a sea creature swam around her but forgetting she was under the sea she just swallowed water.

At that moment a dolphin put his head under her arm, nudging her upward. Instinctively knowing it was safe, Caron clung tightly to the creature, and as they broke to the surface, she took deep gasps of air, coughing up the salty water.

"Oh, thank you!" she spluttered, as she emerged in a pod of dolphins.

These creatures were known to be kindly animals, who often frolicked around in the waters of Portmer. The one she clutched whistled at her with a strange noise that she had never heard before. She guessed it was dolphin language.

By kicking her feet and paddling her arms, Caron realised she could stay afloat, even if she had to hold on to one of them with a paw.

"Hey, if only Braith could see me! I'm swimming."

Now she was safe was drowning, Caron looked around her and gasped. The Human ships were fast approaching! "Gentle Friga!"

At that point, another dolphin came up behind Caron and nudged her bottom.

"Don't do that," she yelped, worried she would drop back into the sea once more. However, the creature did it again, this time half pushing her onto the first dolphin's back. "Oh, you want me to climb on top." With trepidation, she did as they wanted and clung tightly to its fin, terrified she would slip off. But as others came in close, as they provided a safety net of bodies if she should fall, and she felt safe.

The pod set off. Caron tensed as they got faster. The water splashed around her and the salt air stung her cheeks but for all that, she found it rather exhilarating.

Beginning to relax, she glanced around and saw they were outdistancing the enemy ships.

"Good!" Except what should she do next? Leaning forward she tried talking to the dolphins, shouting over the wind as it whistled past. "Can you take me to Portmer?"

She repeated herself. There was no response, other than a trill which may or may not mean them saying yes. There wasn't much she could do other than sit tight.

When they rounded the headland and approached the Port where the Lyon fisher-folk lived, Caron cursed. There were more than just Lyon ships. Human ships had got there before her! Some must have been ahead when she had fallen into the water without her realising.

Even the dolphins were apprehensive as they slowed down, veering away from land.

"Whatever shall we do?" She could ask them to take her back to Whitesands Bay or any of the coves on the far side where the Merfolk lived. On this part of the Isle, after the Port, there were just steep cliffs.

Suddenly the creatures started swimming fast. Caron glanced around, wondering if they had been alerted by danger, but no enemy ships were close by. Did the dolphins have a plan?

CHAPTER THREE

Fleeing from the Humans

Braith had been playing a merry game skimming the waves on his way home, riding the crest, then flipping his tail underneath him just before the surf crashed to land back in the deeper water.

Usually he played this game with the dolphins, but there were none about, which was slightly strange as this was their favourite spot.

He was very happy even if the creatures were absent. He had completed the Quest with Caron and Nia and they had found all the pieces of the crown. The Merboy then contemplated exactly what the Lyon-Lord would do with it and how it was supposed to save them from the Humans.

Another wave came, interrupting his thoughts. It was bigger than usual. Braith lay flat along it, grinning with glee, loving the spray of water on his face and the bubbling of water beneath his stomach as the wave gathered pace.

Relaxing back in the water he glanced up to the cliff, grinning at Caron and Nia on the path waving at him.

The Merboy signalled back and was slightly bemused when Caron kept on flapping her arms. He frowned. She seemed to be indicating something and he turned around in time to get splashed right in the face by the surf.

He was too astonished by what he saw to worry about being hurt. For coming up on him very fast was a ship!

"That's not a fisher ship!" Some of the Lyon-people were fisher-folk, but their ships were much smaller. Who in all the seas could it be?

As he hesitated for a moment, someone from the ship leant over pointing in his direction.

"THERE'S ONE OF THEM!"

It was a Human!

Swimming quickly out of the way to avoid being run down by the ship, the Merboy then realised he had a bigger problem. The man held a spear—and he was aiming it at Braith!

Diving down into the water, he wiggled his tail quickly to come under the other side of the ship, hoping this would confuse the Humans. Unfortunately, as his head broke to the surface Braith found himself amongst several more enemy ships all moving fast.

"In all the depths!" To evade the vessels, the Merboy swam as quickly as he could, trying to outdistance them, but they were nearly as speedy as he. Braith was also wondering how he could get away from them, since they seemed to all be going the same way—and it wasn't where he wanted to go. Taking a moment to think, Braith realised they were probably making for Portmer and he sincerely hoped that Caron and Nia were able to warn their people.

I need to get to Grandmaid and tell the Merfolk!

To do that he needed to double back. The caves the Merfolk lived in were on the other side of the Isle. With his lungs heaving from the extended effort, Braith decided to try turning around. The danger was, that he'd get struck by one of the ships.

So instead he veered off into the shallower channel close to Cove Shore that they were now passing, hoping the ships couldn't get in that close. By doing so, he could swim in the opposite direction.

Just in time. A spear came whizzing past his ear, slowing as it fell into the water. He ducked under the surface just as another came, nicking his tail, causing Braith to grimace in pain as he moved further into the shallows, desperately trying to find some way to turn around and get back to the Merfolk.

Too late! A Human ship came straight at him, ploughing the water in front, causing a wave to surge at him. His lungs hurt from staying underneath the water. He could do nothing other than swim the crest of the wave as it crashed toward land, his arms flailing around as he washed onto the sand like a beached whale.

Braith took deep gulps. As he lay trembling and sore, he noticed with horror that the ship that had chased him had landed on the beach further down!

"I can't stay here!" he cried to himself, watching as Humans poured over the side of their ship, carrying swords and spears. He'd never seen one of them before. They had long untidy dark hair, and heavy bodies. Some ran to the cliffs and started climbing them, some ran down the beach the other way…but some came straight at him! He didn't think they had come to say hello. The enemy were known for taking Merfolk captive—or worse.

"Uh oh. I've got to get away." But as he glanced at the sea, there were too many ships in the water. He couldn't go back that way. He looked around the beach swiftly, searching for a place to hide, hoping to find a boulder to duck behind until the ships had passed by. Then he noticed the Coral Cave that they had explored earlier. Remembering Caron and Nia had found a way out the back, he got excited. Before he could even think about it…the scales on his tail started dissolving, sprinkling onto the sand like tiny granules of silver leaving behind legs. Honest-to-goodness legs!!

The Merboy gasped.

"There it is! Let's get it," yelled a Human striding quickly in his direction.

Braith didn't have time to admire his legs. He needed to get out of there—fast!

CHAPTER FOUR

Warning!

Rees smiled indulgently at Nia. "Whatever are you talking about? Have you been playing 'pretend' with the other Fairies?"

Nia gritted her teeth. "NO! It's for real!"

The Ruler of the Fae narrowed his eyes. "You are normally a sensible child. If you are playing tricks, Nia...."

"I'm not!"

Her uncle took hold of her shoulders. "Where did you see them?"

She pointed back the way she came. "At the look-out point. There were hundreds of ships sailing right toward us!"

Rees stared intently at her face for a moment then turned away from her. Nia was the pleased by how fast her uncle responded, sending some men to the villages to help the Lyon-people and some men to the far side of the forests to make sure no Humans came that way. He turned to the Fairy standing next to him. "Morwenna, go to the stone temple and retrieve the crown. The other parts may be found already. Go swiftly. There's no time to lose."

Nia bit her lip and urgently tugged at her uncle's arm trying to get his attention.

"Shh, Nia."

"Uncle!"

"You'll be safe, I promise you, Nia. But we have work to do."

"WILL YOU LISTEN TO ME!" she yelled and was astonished when all the Fae in the clearing turned to face her, including Morwenna. She nearly laughed at the astonished expressions on their faces, except this was too serious. In a quieter voice, she continued, "We already have the crown from the temple."

"What?! I don't understand. How could you know about—" The Ruler of the Fae was dumbfounded.

Nia fidgeted. "Well, we went on the Quest to find the Lost Crown mentioned in the prophecy and found it."

Rees took hold of her shoulders once more, his fingers tightening. "This is vital, Nia. Where did you put it?"

She frowned. "With the other pieces."

Her uncle's jaw dropped in utter amazement. "Y-you have ALL the pieces?"

Nia nodded.

"Including the one the Merfolk have? And the Lyons' third of the crown? And the *emerald*?"

She nodded each time.

Rees stood up, running a hand through his long straight ash-blond hair. "But how did you get them?"

The Fairy then quickly—and briefly—told her uncle about making friends with the Lyon-girl and the Merboy and all their adventures.

Her uncle smiled softly. "You were always the clever one, Nia. Always reading books. I'm not surprised it was you who completed the Quest."

The Fairy blushed. "But it wasn't just me. It was Caron and Braith, too, and now Caron has the crown. I last saw her going toward Portmer."

He shook his head sadly. "It's possible she's been captured if the Humans are as close as you said."

Nia made a face. She was sure that neither Caron nor Braith would allow themselves to be captured. But then *she* was nearly caught in the *Wild Woods*...and a shiver of fear went down her spine.

Rees continued, "We need someone to go to the Castell and tell the Lyon-Lord." He turned to look at the dog, then spoke to the Fae next to him. "Barris, can you ride this hound as fast as you can?"

However, the dog backed away when Barris approached. The Fairy tried again and this time the hound went over to Nia and nudged her body. Nia gasped.

"Hmm," said the Ruler of the Fae, thoughtfully. "Nia, can you ride the creature and warn Leolin?"

"Oh. Yes. I can do that." And she swiftly climbed back on the dog and off they sped.

But it wasn't until they were sprinting over the fields toward the home of the Lyon-Lord that she realised what she was doing. It was one thing to talk to Caron. After all, she was just a child, too. But to actually talk to the Lord of the Lyons! "I can do it. I've escaped from Grifftan and from the *Wild Woods*. I've climbed through caves and up gullies. I can face up to a Lyon."

* * * *

As the dog skidded into the courtyard of the Castell, home to the Lyon-Lords, Nia looked up at the imposing building with its fortress-like roof and swallowed nervously.

Then a Lyon-man came into sight and stopped in his tracks, staring at her in astonishment.

The Fairy opened her mouth to say something, but her mouth was dry. Then the Lyon-man raced inside, calling for the Lyon-Lord.

She started trembling and nearly fainted when Leolin came striding out, his wife, Tegwen, by his side. Befitting his role, he was the tallest Lyon on the Isle, and as he approached Nia, he towered over her.

"Well, well. It isn't often we get a member of the Fae visiting us, and even rarer when we see a Fairy on the back of our hound." The Lyon-Lord's voice was deep but not loud, as if he was trying not to scare her. "How can I help you, little one?"

"Th-the Humans are coming!" Nia spluttered her words, desperate to get them out. "My uncle, Rees, sent me to tell you!"

Tegwen gasped and put a paw to her throat. "Caron! She's out there!"

"Where is she? Where did she go today?" asked the Lyon-Lord, his eyes wide in alarm.

"I know where she is," said Nia in a quiet voice. She jumped when they both twisted around to stare at her. "S-she's on her way back from Coral Cave, where we found the emerald to fit in the crown." As she had their attention, the tale of their Quest tumbled from her lips once more.

Leolin looked extremely worried and turned back to Caron's mother. "This is my worst fear. My child may be lost. And how can we fight them without the crown?"

His wife laid a gentle paw on the Lyon-Lord's chest. Her voice was swollen with tears. "Send word to our people to look out for Caron while I pray to Friga she is unharmed. In the meantime, we will do our best for all the creatures who live here."

Nia watched as Leolin took a ragged breath, then shouted to his men, "Glyn, tell our people to gather any swords and other weapons to defend themselves. Owein, get them to load the cannons. We will ride down the Isle toward Portmer and meet the enemy where we find them."

He then knelt in front of Nia and the hound. "The dog is called Toby. If you can bear riding him again, he will take you home. Thank you, brave Nia. Now fly like the wind."

CHAPTER FIVE

Braith's Legs

Braith was truly frightened. If he stayed on land, he would be caught by the Humans who were landing. He struggled to get to his feet.

"How in all the watery hells do Caron and Nia manage to walk, let alone run or jump?"

He was desperate. There were several men now running toward him. Gathering all the effort he could, he staggered a few wobbly steps, getting faster as he got used to his legs. He was aiming for the cave of the emerald. His legs were hurting him, unused to the effort, but when he stepped on a conch-shell he yowled in pain and fell to the sand.

Limping, he could only make it to a large rock and fell against it. Braith knew he couldn't get to Coral Cave now and escape that way. The Merboy wanted to sob. He couldn't think of anything more he could do! What use were his legs?

But just as he was giving up, a new adversary rose up from behind the rock—the octopus!

In all the seas, where did he come from? Humans on one side, his arch-enemy, the octopus, on the other. Braith didn't stand a chance.

However, instead of squirting him with ink like the octopus usually did, it flattened itself on the shore and stared at Braith with his huge eyes.

"What?" Braith was mystified by the octopus's strange behaviour.

Shouts came from the enemy as they descended on him waving their spears. "Get 'im!" Braith felt sick to the stomach and said a silent goodbye to Caron and Nia.

Then the octopus scuttled closer, and just as one of them reached out to grab Braith it squirted ink at the man's face.

"Arrrrgh! Kill the creature and get the Merboy," yelled the Human as he fell back, wiping his hands over his face.

Braith grinned, but only for a moment. More approached, although somewhat tentatively, holding their spears in throwing position. The Merboy crouched down, protecting his head with his arms.

Then he felt something touch his leg. Looking down, Braith could see it was a tentacle from the octopus, which then wound around Braith's waist and lifted the exhausted boy onto his back.

"What the—," cried the Humans who stood rigid in amazement, their spears dropping down as they watched their prey being taken by the eight-tentacled sea monster.

After Braith got over his astonishment, he grinned at the enemy as the octopus swiftly scuttled over the sand toward the sea, taking Braith with him—away from the ships!

Once back in the water, Braith felt his tail start to reappear and he slid into the sea.

"Thank you. I will never steal anything from you again, kind sir."

He dived down quickly, catching an underwater current, and swam in the direction of the Mercaves. He might have wanted his legs all this time, but he was very relieved to have his tail back.

Braith might have avoided the Humans that had landed on the shore, but he was aware that there were still others about and he darted quicker than a fish avoiding a killer whale.

Finally, the part of the Isle where the Merfolk lived came into sight. This was a series of caves on a sheer cliff. He was just in time as a ship chased him close to the cliff. He could feel the prow of the vessel just inches away as he skidded into his grandmother's cave.

"GRANDMAID!" Braith yelled at the top of his voice as he flung himself onto the reef to the left. His quick action was just in time, as a spear followed him inside.

His grandmother came rushing out of the inner cave just in time to see the metal bound harmlessly off the water. "What in all depths is that?" The elderly Mermaid stood with her hands on her hips, her long grey hair swirling around her calves.

From his position Braith saw the moment that Delyth, the Queen of the Merfolk, became aware of their predicament. Her expression went from annoyed to horrified.

"We need to warn the people. Where is the shell of warning?" cried the Merboy, urgently trying to get his grandmother to act.

For a few moments, Delyth just stared out at the ships passing by. Swimming over to his grandmother, Braith moved up onto the land, his legs coming more easily this time.

Gripping Delyth by her upper arms, he gave a squeeze. "The shell?"

The Queen of the Merfolk lost her astonishment and urgently pulled her grandson into the inner cave. She pointed to an alcove in the cave wall where the precious shell resided. This time Braith could easily reach up and reverently lifted it down. He handed it to her but she shook her head.

Smiling gently, Delyth gestured to him. "You have proven yourself to be a Merman instead of a boy. I think it should be your reward. Blow hard and call our people. Tell them the ancient enemy is at hand."

Braith gripped the shell tightly, not wanting to drop it at this incredibly important moment and have it shatter on the reef he stood on. It was very large and heavy, shaped like a horn with a wide opening at one end and a smaller opening at the other. He blew deeply into the small end, not expecting the high-pitched, tinkling sound that came out, like a million tiny bells ringing at the same time.

He stopped and frowned, wondering how such a sweet noise would get across the water.

Delyth grinned. "It will work. You'll see." Braith handed the shell back to his grandmother. "Now, go to the Merhall and join our folk. It's time for action!"

CHAPTER SIX

The Dolphins' Plan

Caron soon guessed the dolphins' plan as they swam straight toward the sheer cliffs on the other side of the port.

"I can't climb up there!"

But then she saw where they were making for. It was covered steps that went up the cliff face in a zig zag. She knew exactly where it came out and also knew instantly that it was the perfect place for her to be. But no Lyon ever ascended those steps as they had been made by Fairies long ago. They were just too narrow.

However, the dolphins were determined to drop her off at that place. Not that there were many other options, as the rest of the Isle was surrounded by steep cliffs. She couldn't go back to Whitesands Bay—not with the Humans coming from that direction—and Portmer was clearly out of the question.

As she cautiously clambered off the dolphin onto the steps, trying to avoid slipping into the water, Caron was slightly relieved to be on land again and waved her rescuers goodbye, but was she stranded there?

Turning to face the stairs, Caron tried stepping on the first one, testing it for her weight. She saw that if she went on tiptoe, she could climb the steps. "I can do this if I go carefully." Except she really wanted to hurry! She had to warn her people. At least this route would bring her out at the bottom of the Bell Tower.

Moving one step at a time, she made her way up, thanking whoever it was that decided to have landing places here and there, so she could rest.

It was at one of these stopping points that she looked out of an opening and saw the bulk of the ships descending on Portmer. "Come on, Caron! You must go quicker!"

She turned to the final ascent and made her way up the steep steps, her calves burning with agony.

Finally, she burst onto the top of the cliff. She was there! She had reached Government Green. This was where the Lyon-men held their main councils, but today was a rest day and no-one was about, however, it didn't matter as she knew exactly where she had to go.

Ignoring the pain in her legs, she quickly ran to the Bell Tower, skidding to a halt at the bottom of the steps. It was just as she remembered. The door to the ancient tower was blocked by a chain. As long as she could remember, this doorway had been closed. But it wasn't a simple chain. It covered the door like a giant spider's web, and anyone attempting to touch it was repelled as if it was a force field. She knew because she—and every other Lyon-child—had tried.

She had asked her mother one time why the Bell Tower was chained, but Tegwen had only said, "When the time is right, the chain will be released." It all sounded rather mysterious in Caron's opinion and her mother had smiled. "If the bell was rung all the time, the people would just think it was an everyday happening, instead of something important."

"And this is SOOOO important, surely it must open now," Caron said out loud as she slowly climbed the few steps to the door. The force tried to push her away. She gritted her teeth, trying once more, but was still unsuccessful. "Oh, Friga! Please. I have to warn the people."

Stepping back to gather herself for another assault, Caron felt the sword bang her thigh and inspiration hit her.

"That's what the sword is for!" she cried. "Thank Friga, I still have it!"

Unsheathing the blade, the Lyon-girl turned it on its side to read the words again.

CUT THE MAGICAL CHAIN

"It MUST mean *this* chain. Why didn't I think of it before?" she chided herself. But then the Humans had only just arrived, so it wouldn't have been necessary to ring the bell before.

Gripping the sword in both paws, the Lyon-girl raised it high over her head and brought it down on the chain with one almighty heave.

She fully expected it to rebound off the chain and throw her to the ground. But when the chain splintered into tiny fragments like glass, she gasped. "Friga! I did it!"

Putting the sword away, Caron reached out a tentative paw and pushed at the door, which opened with a creak. Her lethargy dissipated, and she charged inside, only stopping when she saw there were circular steps up the tower.

"Not more steps!" At least these were the right size for Lyon feet.

She quickly ran up them, coming into a room at the top where she saw a rope hanging down from the bell.

This room had windows looking out each side. Caron rushed to the side that overlooked the sea and noticed with horror that more Human ships were approaching Portmer. But she grinned as she then saw whales, dolphins and Merfolk swimming toward them and correctly guessed the Merboy had warned his people. "Well done, Braith!"

Running to the other side of the tower, she looked out trying to see the forest in the far distance, hoping Nia had been equally successful. It wasn't that easy to see, as it was too far off, but for an instant she thought she saw a giant dog with a Fairy on its back. "No, it can't be. That wasn't Nia, was it?"

The Lyon-girl had no time to ponder on her friends, as she spied hordes of men swarming up the hill from Portmer. There was no time to lose. She had to warn her people.

Taking hold of the rope, Caron pulled with all her might and the bell boomed deep and loud. It hurt her ears, but she couldn't stop now and pulled it again and again. When she finally stopped, the motion of the rope made the bell continue ringing for a bit. Caron sprinted back down the steps.

The people of Lyon Isle were now warned. But the Humans wouldn't be defeated until she got the crown to her father.

CHAPTER SEVEN
Shelter Valley

This time Toby took Nia back to the woods via the village of Chantry. She would have been amused by the stares of the Lyon-people as she passed if the situation hadn't been so desperate.

As they neared the pond with the statue of a Mermaid at the edge of the forest, she saw a Human! He was threatening some Merchildren with his spear.

"Oh no!" she cried. "We must do something." But what could a little Fairy and a giant dog do? She wished she had kept the sword now.

But Toby knew exactly what to do. Charging at the man, he leapt up and bit the Human's backside!

Nia was totally flabbergasted and had to hold on tight as Toby landed on the ground. She was very afraid the Human would retaliate but started laughing as the man dropped his spear, clutched his bottom and ran away screaming.

She sat up on Toby, so she could talk to the Merchildren. "They could come back. Can you get out and come with me into the woods to safety?"

The eldest Merchild answered. "Unfortunately, most of us haven't got our legs yet. We aren't normally allowed to come this far up the island, but we were swimming away from the men."

Nia thought for a moment. "Then can you hide in the tunnels?" She knew from Braith that there were underground passageways from the various ponds around the Isle that led down to the sea. When the Merchildren said they would do that, the Fairy jumped down and lugged the abandoned spear over to the first Merchild. "Here. Take this just in case any Humans try crawling down the tunnel."

She then climbed on Toby once more, and as they moved away from the village into the woods, she started to hear a strange ringing sound.

"Stop, please."

Toby skidded to a halt, almost flinging Nia onto the ground.

The Fairy grunted and sat up. As useful as Toby had been, Nia would be very happy when this was over and she could get down. She frowned at the noise. "What is it?" Then she gasped. She was pretty sure it was coming from the chained Bell Tower high on the cliffs, although she'd never heard the bell before. At that moment, she realised why the sword so was important. It was one of the tales she had forgotten.

Nia slapped her forehead. "Of course. Why didn't I remember that?" Then it occurred to her that it must be Caron ringing the bell.

"Yay! Caron did it! She cut the chains!" Nia was extremely pleased, because this also meant that Caron hadn't been captured by the Humans.

Immediately, Nia was surrounded by many Fae, including her uncle Rees.

"I did it! I told Leolin," she shouted to them.

The Ruler of the Fae clasped her arm. "Well done, child. The bell will warn all the other Lyon-people across the Isle. I also heard the Merfolk are in action." Nia was glad, as that meant Braith had got back home, too.

"There is one more thing to do," Rees said.

As Nia watched, her uncle blew on the horn that he always carried, and within seconds the elusive Unicorn appeared.

Shimmering fairydust! The creature was as beautiful as Caron had mentioned.

Rees spoke to the Unicorn. "Please stay with Nia and gather all the children you can find hereabouts—Lyons, Mer, Fae and any other young creatures. Take them to Shelter Valley in the centre of the forest. They will be safe there. We will go to the cliffs and drive the Humans into the *Wild Woods*."

Nia shivered. She now knew how dangerous that place was.

As all the adult Fae raced off to deal with any Humans venturing into the forest, the Unicorn reared up onto two legs and neighed—it was a light, chiming sound, almost like a song. Nia felt warm and happy and had a strong desire to follow the creature. Immediately, some Fae children came running out of the woods looking startled to see Nia on the back of a giant dog. She waved them over.

"C—can we join you?" Nia turned her head and saw some anxious Lyon-children next. They had ventured from the nearby village. It was strange to see them looking frightened. It was usually the Fae who were fearful of the scary Lyons.

"Of course. Please come. We will keep you safe." And to her astonishment the Unicorn bent one leg so they could put the younger children on its back. And then they set off, Fae and Lyons walking side by side.

They hadn't gone far when some more Lyon-children ran after them. "Wait for us!" To her astonishment, some carried Merchildren they had rescued.

She smiled. "That's good. We'll be safe if we stay together."

Nia was amazed at how many other children they found on the way. She couldn't believe that all the people of the Isle were gathering in the same place, no longer afraid of each other. They headed for the forest, collecting some baby foxes, bunnies and hedgehogs along the way. And as they passed the lake in the next valley, not far from the temple where she had vanished from, some Merchildren waved.

"Come," she shouted. "We are going to safety." Some of the aquatic beings managed to shed their tails and walk. Others were helped onto the back of the Unicorn or carried by Lyons.

Finally, they climbed over the brow of a hill and through a narrow gorge to reach Shelter Valley, where Nia's mother and other adult Fae were waiting to welcome them with lanterns to light their way.

Nia looked back at the line of young beings of Lyon Isle, proud that she had helped save them. It reminded her of Caron and Braith, and she hoped they were safe, too.

CHAPTER EIGHT

Into Battle

When the bell rang, Braith heard a noise in his ears like he had been hit on the head. He shook himself vigorously and his hair slapped around his face. However, he could still hear the ringing and wondered where it was coming from.

Braith had been astonished at how quickly the Merfolk gathered themselves to fight. Even more astounding had been the fact that other sea creatures had been waiting for them when they emerged from the Mercaves—the sea was filled with whales, dolphins, seals and other beings.

His grandmother came alongside him. "Good. The shell called them to battle, too. This is *our* island, *our* seas. We won't let anyone take it from us."

There had been battle with Human ships already as they swam into action, with the whales using their magnificent bodies to crash into the enemy boats. Braith yelled excitedly as he and other Merfolk climbed on board the creatures or swam speedily alongside to catch up with the ships ahead.

The Merboy was worried, though, that the ships that had forced him onto the shore had now landed and were taking over the Isle.

"Go faster!" he yelled. "We need to get to Portmer."

As they passed the headland, Braith looked up at the cliff in the distance and saw the Bell Tower, suddenly realising that's where the ringing had come from. Braith grinned and raised a fist in the air, guessing it was the Lyon-girl's doing. "Way to go, Caron!"

But something even more amazing happened next. Firstly, came a new sound, like an axe on stone, which set Braith's teeth on edge. As the Merboy and his friends turned to the new noise, he could tell it was coming from the enormous stone ship at Portmer which creaked agonisingly. All at once, it broke apart—but it wasn't wrecked! Instead, it was a wooden ship once more, the stone falling into the water with loud thuds, causing a rush of waves. The tale of why the ship, *Amis*, had turned to stone was lost in time. Maybe Nia knew it, Braith pondered, but now wasn't the time, as a huge wave caused by the stone crashing into the sea came hurtling toward him.

Braith was used to choppy water and rode it easily, unlike the Human ships swarming in the bay, which were toppling about, trying to stay upright. The army of Merfolk and their sea friends swam in between the enemy ships to get close to Portmer.

He grimaced when he saw some ships had already landed and smoke rose up from buildings they had set alight. The Lyon-men and Fae would have to deal with that, but the Merfolk and their friends could try to stop more of them getting on to their Isle.

A cheer went up from the Lyon-men who were fighting on the quay and they swarmed onto the once-mighty ship, *Amis*, quickly raising its orange triangular sails as the smaller fishing vessels came alongside, already battered from their combat.

Then the *Amis* steamed past Braith as he rode the swell, and he shouted with glee.

"*Amis*! *Amis*! *Amis*!"

He chuckled as he saw the Human ships start to falter against the tide of Lyon ships bearing down on them led by the *Amis,* which was twice their size.

As Braith watched, despite cannon balls coming from the cannons on the cliff tops thundering down around them, the battle appeared even. Neither side gaining an advantage such was the size of the Human force. He grimaced and swiftly looked around to see what he could do to help. Something he saw gave him an idea. Flicking his tail swiftly, he dived under the water, gaining speed, and sprang onto the netting over the side of the *Amis*.

"Hey!" he called, trying to attract the attention of the Lyons on board the ship. He called again but knew he couldn't be heard over the roar of the battle. Braith closed his eyes tightly and tried to think legs, gasping as he felt his scales fall away.

The change was so sudden the Merboy cried as he slid down the netting. Gripping tightly, Braith hung on and lifted a leg to climb.

He was sweating hard, but he managed to get to the top and called again.

A startled Lyon-man looked over at him. Braith knew him, as he'd stolen fish from Elson's nets in the past. If he got out of this, he knew he would never steal again.

"Elson!" Braith shouted. "Drive them onto Grifftan!" He pointed firmly in the direction of the mysterious island which had just appeared to his right.

The Lyon-man raised a paw, indicating he knew exactly what Braith meant, and raised his voice to give the order.

Happy that his idea was going to be implemented, Braith jumped off the net back into the water, landing with a splash in the middle of a pod of Merfolk, with his tail back once more.

It looked like every single one of his people was out in force, keeping pace with the flotilla of boats led by the Lyon-men.

Within minutes, their boats tacked against the wind, causing the Human ships to veer toward Grifftan. Even the weather appeared to be on their side, the wind shifting to help them. Then came a grinding noise as one enemy ship hit the rocks around the little island, and then another. Men jumped out, trying to escape their sinking ships, yelling angrily at the Lyons.

Some even tried to swim across the channel to Lyon Isle, but Braith and his people formed a line, snapping their strong tails at any foolhardy Human attempting this.

A few enemy ships barely managed to avoid crashing into the island and fled back to the mainland when they could see there was no way past all the sea folk or Lyon-ships.

"Good riddance! Never come back!" cried Braith.

Of course, none of the Lyon-ships had any problems. They knew where the rocks were and avoided them, standing guard offshore, waiting.

And then it happened. Mist came over the island and it started to disappear. As Braith listened, the angry yells of the Humans changed into anxious screams. Soon the mist covered the island totally and it disappeared, taking them to their doom.

"Let's go. We need to check the other side of the Isle," shouted Elson. "Thank you, good Merfolk."

While the *Amis* sailed around the coastline, the other Lyon-ships sailed back to port to help with the skirmish on land. Meanwhile, the whales stayed in the bay in case any more Human vessels should appear.

Braith felt proud of the battle they had just fought, but his thoughts then turned to his friends. What was happening with Caron and Nia?

CHAPTER NINE
The Colonnade

Caron got down from the Bell Tower just in time. Humans armed with swords were running uphill from Lady Square. They grappled with the Lyons who were manning the cannons on the clifftops. They would get to her next!

She had rung the bell to warn the people of Lyon Isle, but if the prophecy was correct, she had to get the crown to her father. Except he was likely to be on the other side of the island in their home at the Castell.

As she bit her claw, Caron wished Nia and Braith were with her to decide what to do. At least they were likely to be safely in the sea and the woods, she thought. Caron felt a huge sense of achievement that was instantly tinged with sorrow that she had not gone on the Quest earlier.

"First things first. I have to get away from here."

Darting in the opposite direction from the oncoming Humans, Caron took a little-used back path down the hill toward the herb garden and the lion statue.

Thankfully she didn't come across any more men.

Caron hesitated by the statue. "What do I do now?" The quickest route home was via the road past the Bell Tower, only enemies were already there. "If they are at the Port, they've probably got to the Inn at Trinity Row, so I can't go there and get a lift in a cart."

She decided to make for the watermill in the first instance that she had used to hide from Graham and his friends. That seemed a long time ago now. The Lyon-girl started to stride in that direction. If she encountered any Humans, she could shelter in there. As Caron hurried along an idea came to her. If she crept through the herb gardens she could make her way to the Colonnade. This was a ruined building, originally built by the first Lyon-Lord, but she knew a secret passageway went from there to the village of Chantry. Then she could run across the fields to the Castell. Surely the Humans hadn't got that far on to the Island?

Although the Lyon-girl could hear distant sounds of cannons booming, and voices yelling, she moved very stealthily through the herbs and encountered no-one. Relieved to have got that far, Caron began to hear fighting close by and hurriedly went to the third corbel along the top. These were stone figurines of animals that lived on the Isle, apart from the third one which was a Lyon-man. She knew by turning it to the left, that it opened the secret passage—she had done it in the past after finding out about it in an old book.

Just as Caron reached up to the corbel, she heard a noise and whirled around, thinking there must be a Human near her. Nothing. She frowned and turned back to the figure, then stopped as she heard the sound again. It was someone sobbing!

Walking around the pillar Caron spied someone huddled at the far end. When she got closer and saw who it was, she hesitated. "Graham?"

Her brother lifted his head. "Caron, what are you doing here?" Then he jumped to his feet and looked around wildly. "The Humans are here."

Caron's heart thumped in her chest and she twirled around looking for other people but then became aware that he was referring to the enemy being in the Isle. "Yes, I know."

However, she wasn't expecting Graham's next statement. "It's all my fault they came!"

"What??"

He slumped on a low stone wall. "I told my uncle where we were!"

Caron couldn't believe her ears and sat down next to her brother, confused by what he was telling her. "I don't understand. I know you are half Human, Graham, but I didn't know you had an uncle."

Her brother then explained. "You are aware that Mother was on a ship that was wrecked on the mainland. Some Humans took her in—they can be nice people! She was rescued by the Lyons after a while, and by then she'd had me." Caron nodded. "Well, there was an agreement that every year she or another Lyon would bring me to visit my father's family."

The Lyon-girl knew that her brother went off for a trip each year but had presumed he just went sailing.

"So, I was at my uncle's a month ago—my father died when I was a baby—and he asked me how long it took to sail to Lyon Isle and in which direction."

Caron's stomach rolled anxiously as she listened to her brother's tale.

"He also asked about a crown that belonged to the Lyon-Lord, but I said we didn't have any crowns." Graham shrugged.

No, but I do, thought Caron.

She jumped to her feet and strode back to the pillar she had been working on. "It's vital I get to father. I have a way of saving the Isle."

Graham goggled at his sister. "How?"

"There's no time to explain. I'm going to open the secret tunnel and go up to Chantry."

"But he's not there." Graham had joined Caron. "I ran off when a little Fairy on a giant dog came to the Castell to warn Leolin."

The Lyon-girl's jaw dropped. "Gentle Friga. That must have been Nia. Good for her."

"I heard that father was trying to get to Portmer but only got as far as Telcorn. I—I wanted to go with him, but I was scared."

In that moment, Caron was no longer intimidated by her big brother. "Then we must go to Telcorn," she declared strongly. "Instead of going up this tunnel to

Chantry, I'll take the left turning. It will take me along the back of the Colonnade to the Gloriette." This opened in Telcorn, so it was an ideal secret route to avoid the enemy. She reached up to turn the corbel and the wooden door without a lock at the back of the Colonnade creaked open.

Graham's widened in astonishment and stepped back. "I can't go."

Caron didn't have time to persuade him and strode quickly into the dark passageway, moving as fast as she could. It was pitch black, so she had to feel her way by touching the wall on either side.

She hadn't gone far when she heard running behind her.

"Quick, Caron! The Humans are behind us." Noises came from further back...the sounds of people carrying swords, and the two ran as fast as they could, in fear of their lives, occasionally banging into the sides of the tunnel in the dark!

Then the tunnel came to an abrupt end and Caron yelped as she ran into the wall, bruising her nose. Graham nearly ploughed into her, "How do we get out?" he cried fearfully.

Caron was feeling around for a handle. She gave a sigh of relief when she finally found it and the two fell out of the tunnel into the basement of the Gloriette—a barber shop in the village of Telcorn. They slammed the door shut behind them. Just in time! The Humans who had come after them ferociously banged on the door, pushing it, trying to open it.

Graham braced himself to keep it shut. His face showed dismay when he became aware that one of them had to stay and hold it shut. "Go, Caron! I'll stay here."

She hesitated, unsure of his motive.

"GO! Tell Leolin and Mother I love them and … that I'm sorry."

Caron kissed her brother quickly, who, for once, was being brave, and then quickly ran upstairs and out of the Gloriette into the midst of fighting.

CHAPTER TEN

The Battle of Telcorn

As Caron burst out of the building into Telcorn, a village near the entrance to the forest, she skidded to a halt, gasping at the sight before her. Lyons fought with Humans! And one man came in her direction!!

The crown in the bag banged against her as Caron swiftly unsheathed the sword and swung it against the Human facing her.

"Ow!" he cried. Or was it she who yelled? Either way, it gave her the opportunity to slip past him. She started running full pelt. Her people may have run on four legs many thousands of years ago, but they'd lost that ability now. However, her legs were strong, and she ran like the wind toward her father, who she spied up ahead.

Leolin's voice carried over the sounds of fighting, "Courage, Lyons! This is our island. Don't let them have it! Watch out, Dylan! Owein, close that gap! They mustn't get to the woods."

Caron felt pride in her father and in her people. They may be a peaceful people, but when it came down to it, they were prepared to risk their lives for the gentler creatures of the Isle.

"Got ya!" The Lyon-girl's flight ended abruptly as a Human suddenly grabbed her shoulders, causing her to lose her footing and bang into him, dropping her sword in the process.

Her first thought was rather bizarre—that her enemy wasn't much taller than her. In fact, the Lyons topped all the men they fought, but there were just so many Humans swarming over the village.

"Where do you think you are going?" His breath revolted her, stinking of teeth rotted with sweets. As she turned her head away from him, a thought came to her. Lyons might have lost their animal ability to run on four legs, but they still had sharp teeth. Without waiting another second, she opened her mouth and bit deeply into the hand that held her shoulder.

The Human's yell deafened her, but her trick worked, and he let go. Ducking under his arm, Caron sprinted away, glancing around for her father. Leolin noticed her at the same time and Caron saw the horror in his eyes that his daughter was in the thick of the fighting.

It was only a brief glance as another man barred her way. Caron raised her arm, then swore as she recalled losing her sword. "Oh, Friga!" The Human gave her an evil grin and raised his dagger.

Caron used the only thing she had at hand, the bag with the crown. She swiftly pulled it from her back and swung it at his head. The Human was taken unawares, presumably thinking she was unarmed, and he toppled to the ground. The Lyon-girl murmured to herself, "I hope I haven't broken the crown." But she didn't have time to find out.

Running to the stables, she ducked into the doorway, looking at the mass of bodies fighting, scared that the Lyons appeared to be pushed back by the mass of Humans. She had to do something soon, particularly as two of them, noticing her hiding place, moved menacingly toward her.

Gathering all her strength, she charged at them. The Humans hadn't been expecting that and, as they fell to the ground, she vaulted over them, fear giving her adrenaline. Weaving in between the fighters, she made for the last place she had seen her father.

Her chest was heaving with exertion as she came within touching distance of her, but she groaned as she became aware there was no way of reaching him—he was surrounded by the enemy.

"Father!" she cried in anguish. He looked in her direction, despair etched on his face.

"Caron, get away if you can. I love you."

That gave her a last spurt of courage. Pulling the crown from the bag, she held it tightly in one paw as she gave an almighty dive forward, sliding under the legs of the people fighting around her father, knocking some off their feet. She got kicked and scraped, but her slide took her to her father's feet. "Take it! Here's the crown."

"Well done, child!"

Leolin didn't waste another second and, taking the crown from his daughter's outstretched paw, he raised it over his head.

He cried in a loud, gruff voice, "ENOUGH!"

"No!" yelled the closest Human.

"Get 'im before he puts it on!"

But it was too late. Leolin lowered the crown until it sat firmly on his head.

Caron lay there wondering what was going to happen next. Would they just put their bows and swords down? Would they continue fighting?

Neither happened. As she watched, the emerald got brighter and brighter, emitting a green light that shone far and wide. As it went over any Humans, they crumpled and fell to the ground. All the Lyons were stunned at the sudden end to the fighting, then a colossal cheer went up!

Caron gasped as she stood up. "Father, what happened? Are they dead?" As much as she wanted to get rid of them, the thought of them being killed because she had fulfilled the Quest made her a little queasy.

The Lyon-Lord patted his daughter's shoulder as he pulled her into his arms. "Your attitude does you credit. No, my child. They are just unconscious."

She sighed. The Lyon-girl could hardly believe it was over!

After the Lyon people finished cheering, Leolin told everyone to tie the Humans' hands and put them into their boats.

This took a while, and many of the enemy were coming around, cursing and yelling. Whenever the Lyon-Lord went over to them, they quelled and quietened down, muttering beneath their breath.

By then other Lyons had arrived including Tegwen, who clasped her daughter tightly in her arms.

"We will not kill you," declared the Lyon-Lord to the Humans after they had finished leading them back to their boats. "Instead we will leave you some knives to release your restraints. The whales will tow you out to sea. Never come near these shores again or the next time will be worse. Far worse!"

There was still a problem. Being half Human, Graham had also fallen to the ground in the Gloriette, although he had recovered quicker than the others. He stayed to the back now, looking stunned. He clearly didn't know where his place was—with the Lyons or Humans.

Leolin gestured for him to come close. Graham hung his head low. Cupping his step-son's chin, Caron's father asked, "Did you bring them to Lyon Isle, Graham? Why? I have loved you as a son all these years."

Caron hugged her mother who was sobbing. The Lyon-girl felt conflicted. Graham was her brother even if he had been mean to her all her life.

"I—I'm sorry. My Human uncle asked me lots of questions about the Isle and the people and the crown. I told him we didn't have it anymore. I didn't ask them to come."

Caron spoke up at that point. "Graham came to my rescue when I was trying to find you, Father."

The Lyon-Lord glanced at his daughter and smiled. "It seems you redeemed yourself, my son, even if you hadn't meant it to happen in the first place. You can stay—if you help rebuild the homes that were destroyed by the Humans. We will all help."

CHAPTER ELEVEN
Triumphal Arch

"Let's greet our three wonderful children!" cried the Lord of Lyon Isle to the crowds gathered in the centre of Telcorn some days later. "Without them, we would not now be here. Instead, we would be enslaved by the Humans as were our ancestors."

He beckoned them forward. Nia and Caron tightly clutched Braith's hands and the three friends stepped out of the crowd to stand before the Lyon-Lord.

It was a week after the battle, and everything was beginning to get back to normal. The Lyons had returned to their homes, the Merfolk to their caves, the Fae to the woods—and there was no sign of any Human. But now they had all come together once more.

As the three Questers stood surrounded by Lyon-Men, Fae and Merfolk and various other creatures, including the giant dog that had rescued her, Nia reflected on all that had happened—how they had used their ingenuity to find all the pieces of the crown, then battled to warn their peoples, and overcome their own personal obstacles. Caron had shown her father she was worthy of his consideration—a true Lyon-Lady to come. Braith had overcome his laziness and found his legs. As for Nia, she was still astonished at how courageous she had been, from talking to Caron that first time at the wishing tree, to escaping Grifftan, climbing out of caves, entering the *Wild Woods*, riding atop a giant hound, and warning all the people.

Caron was holding tight to Braith. He was still finding it a little hard to walk. Nia squeezed his other hand.

Leolin wore the crown they had found. He stood in front of the gateway to the forest where a new archway was being built at the edge of the village of Telcorn. This was where some children had fled into the woods to join Nia's band of survivors going to Shelter Valley. This had also been the site of the final battle and still bore the signs of the fierce battle that had taken place.

"Come, children," called Leolin. "It is fitting that we should congratulate you here by the Triumphal Arch. You are truly children of the Isle and I commend you on your cleverness and bravery.

"After talking to all the peoples who live here, I am aware that each of you children have had your own personal quests in addition to the Quest for the Lost Crown."

Nia glanced at Braith and then at Caron.

The Fairy was so busy looking at her friends she didn't notice that Leolin had moved to stand in front of her and she jumped when he spoke.

"Little Nia. Your uncle, Rees, ruler of the Fae, tells me you were so quiet and shy that you kept to yourself, missing out on many Fairy events. This was such a shame, as you are very clever and have a lot of knowledge to pass on to others. You overcame this to work with children from the other people on this Isle to find the crown. But, in addition, you brought us word and helped all the young to safety. You are a true Fairy and, although you are not destined to lead the Fae, you will be a great teacher one day."

Nia was so overcome she nearly fainted until a tug from Braith reminded her she was with friends.

"Braith," Leolin took a step toward the Merboy, "your grandmother, Delyth, told me before this you were funny and liked by everyone, but had yet to achieve your legs, despite being of an age to do so."

The Fairy clasped Braith's hand, reassuring him. He was using his legs now, but they were covered with a colourful turquoise sarong. Not that he needed to—the people of the Isle didn't care whether anyone was naked or clothed. It was the Humans who had laws about being nude. Probably because they were so filthy, the Fairy thought. But sometimes a person just wanted to wear something for the occasion and all three of them had their best outfits on—Nia wore a new pale pink dress and Caron her best gold tunic she usually wore on festival days.

The Lyon-Lord was continuing. "The one thing you needed was a purpose, and you certainly gained that, helping save all creatures of the sea and those on land as well as leading a fleet of sea creatures. You are a true Merman and, although you would never be King of the Merfolk, you will be a great general one day."

Nia was so pleased for Braith she hugged his arm. The Merboy just looked stunned.

Leolin stepped in front of his daughter.

"Caron, pride of my life. All along you wanted to prove yourself and I never gave you the opportunity. For that I am very sorry. I dismissed you as too young. But you weren't. Without you, the crown would be languishing in pieces and the battle lost."

He smiled. "And without each of you bringing warning to us, including Caron gaining entrance to the Bell Tower, the Humans would have taken over the Isle. But you, my wonderful daughter, led your fine band of Questers to victory. I will never dismiss you again."

Braith nudged Nia and grinned at her as they both watched Caron beam with joy.

Leolin raised his voice to the crowd. "Behold, the fine Questers!"

The Unicorn then trotted through the crowd to stand in front of the three children. To Nia's amazement, it knelt, bowing before them.

"Gentle Goddess Friga," cried Caron.

Then the Lyon-Lord went down on one knee.

"In all the seas!" breathed Braith in awe.

Finally, everyone else—Lyons, Mer, Fae and all other creatures present—bowed.

"Shimmering fairydust!" Nia gasped. She was so glad that Caron had come to the woods that day and sat on the wishing tree.

CHAPTER TWELVE

The Quest is Over

Braith was sitting on the wishing tree—at least on one part of it, as it had split after Caron's experience. It seemed like a long time ago since the start of their Quest.

"There's one thing I don't understand," he said to the girls. "Was the crown lost or not?"

Caron turned toward the Merboy. "Ah. It turns out they had split the crown into several parts for safety but said it was lost to make sure people didn't look for it. Except they didn't reckon on us!"

They all chuckled at the Lyon-girl's tone of voice.

Nia spoke from her place up a tree. "Apparently they made up the prophecy in case people totally forgot about it when the time came to gather all the pieces."

Although he had his legs, he was slightly envious of the girls. He watched as Nia threw down ripening fruits toward Caron, who was standing below.

He huffed. "Now I have my legs, it's a shame our Quest is over, as I am able to go places with you."

Nia sprang down and ran over to sit on the other part of the tree and Caron followed slowly, looking thoughtful. "I know. I was thinking that myself. But there are still places each of us can go that the others can't."

"What do you mean" he asked.

"Well, Nia is better in the woods and up Fairy steps than I am. There are still dangerous places in the forest even she doesn't like to visit. I am less likely to get stepped on in the villages than you two, as Lyons tend to stride around, and I can reach up higher. And only you can go into watery places, Braith."

"Actually, I was thinking now we have more time I could teach you guys to swim and you can then go places with me." Braith smiled at the others as he lounged on the tree trunk, resting on an elbow. It would be something to do now the Quest was over.

He jumped as a rustling suddenly came from the trees.

"Hey! What's that?" questioned Caron loudly. "It's not a Human, is it?" Before Caron could say anything more, a rabbit rushed out from the bushes, leaping over the wishing tree and down the hill.

They all collapsed in laughter.

"At least you still have your sword, if it had been a man." Braith giggled. The ship called the *Amis* had turned to stone again and the Bell Tower door was once more covered in the magic web of chains. However, Leolin still kept the crown in one piece—just in case any Humans should venture by again.

Caron leapt to her feet and pulled the sword from its sheath. She had been delighted that it had been picked up and handed to her father. Because it had been so important in breaking the chains of the Bell Tower, he only let her wear it occasionally. "Oh yes, I was going to show you. Look, the words have gone." The Lyon-girl displayed the blade to them. It was clear and shiny once more.

"What does that mean?" asked Nia, her eyes wide with surprise. "We already know you can use it on magic chains."

"Maybe there will be a new message if another adventure comes along," said Caron thoughtfully.

Braith sighed and slapped the tree in frustration. "I wish we had another Quest to go on."

Suddenly, the tree he was sitting on split with a loud crack and the Merboy tumbled to the ground.

"Oh no, not again!" Caron rushed over to help Braith to his feet.

"Look," cried Nia. "There's more symbols on the tree!" The other two gasped and swiftly turned to look as Nia read out the Fairy words. "Beware. The woods are dangerous."

Braith snorted. "We already know the *Wild Woods* are treacherous. Look what happened to Nia there."

Nia bit a thumb nail as she pondered. "Generally, the rest of the forest is fine. After all, that's where my people live."

"Hey," cried Caron as more writing appeared on the tree. She knew enough of the Fae language now to translate. "You - must - find - the - magical .... What's that last word, Nia? I can't read it?"

The Fairy looked at it for a moment then stared at the other two. "It says 'potion'."

Braith tried jumping around in glee but ended up falling over with a laugh. "Yay! Another Quest! The Quest for the Magical Potion."

FIND OUT WHAT HAPPENS IN THE NEW QUEST IN THE NEXT BOOK...

THE END

Author Biographies

Joanne Patrick has written many successful adult stories under a different pen-name and this is her first venture into children's stories. Joanne, who lives in York, and has been thrilled to be able to plot the story with her great-niece, Charlotte O'Brien, during their holidays together, and hopes to write many more stories with her.

Charlotte O'Brien will be 14 years old the year we published this and this is her first ever book. She is very excited to share this adventure with her great-aunt along the way. Although she didn't write much of this book (her main contributions being the plotting and some illustrations), she hopes to write more in the future when she has less from school to focus on.

You can connect with Joanne via these methods

Email: Joannepatrick1@yahoo.com

Website:
www.Joannepatrickauthor.blogspot.com

Facebook:
www.facebook.com/joanne.patrick.5492

Three groups of people live on Lyon Isle—the Lyon-men, the Fae, and the Merfolk having arrived on the Isle many generations earlier escaping Humans who wanted to enslave them, but each group rarely talks to each other these days.

When Caron—a Lyon-girl—makes a wish on the wishing tree, she didn't imagine she would become friends with a Fairy called Nia, and Braith, a Merboy. And she certainly didn't expect to go on lots of adventures in the Quest to find the Lost Crown.

Printed in Poland
by Amazon Fulfillment
Poland Sp. z o.o., Wrocław

59565763R00099